SECRET CODERS
Potions & Parameters

GENE LUEN YANG
& MIKE HOLMES

:01
First Second
New York

"It was this wonderful time between magic and so-called rationality."

—Wally Feurzeig, co-creator of the Logo programming language, on the early days of Logo

First Second

New York

Copyright © 2018 by Humble Comics LLC

Published by First Second
First Second is an imprint of Roaring Brook Press,
a division of Holtzbrinck Publishing Holdings Limited Partnership
175 Fifth Avenue, New York, NY 10010

All rights reserved

Library of Congress Control Number: 2017941170

Paperback ISBN: 978-1-62672-607-9
Hardcover ISBN: 978-1-62672-608-6

Our books may be purchased in bulk for promotional, educational,
or business use. Please contact your local bookseller or the Macmillan Corporate
and Premium Sales Department at (800) 221-7945 ext. 5442 or by e-mail at
MacmillanSpecialMarkets@macmillan.com.

First edition, 2018

Book design by Rob Steen

Printed in China by Toppan Leefung Printing Ltd., Dongguan City, Guangdong Province

Paperback: 10 9 8 7 6 5 4 3 2
Hardcover: 10 9 8 7 6 5 4 3 2

BY ART
WE LIVE

Chapter

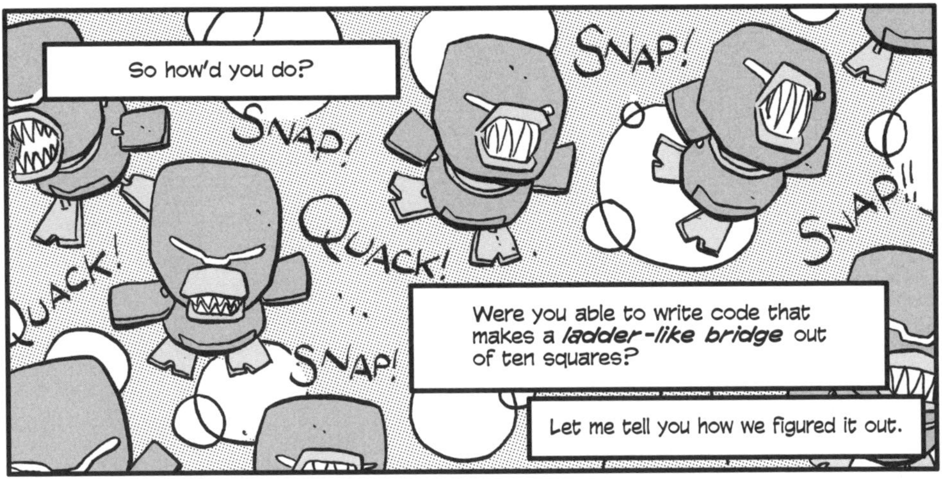
So how'd you do?
SNAP!
SNAP!
QUACK!
QUACK!
SNAP!!
SNAP!
Were you able to write code that makes a *ladder-like bridge* out of ten squares?
Let me tell you how we figured it out.

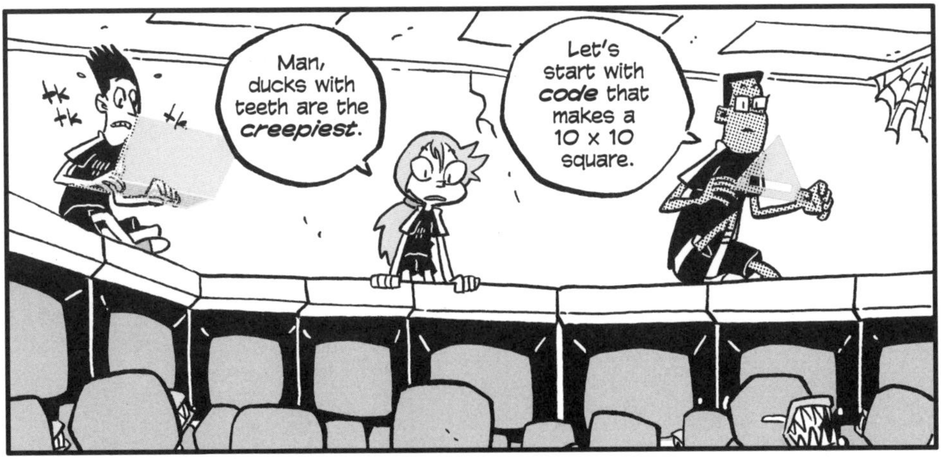
tk tk tk
Man, ducks with teeth are the *creepiest*.
Let's start with *code* that makes a 10 x 10 square.

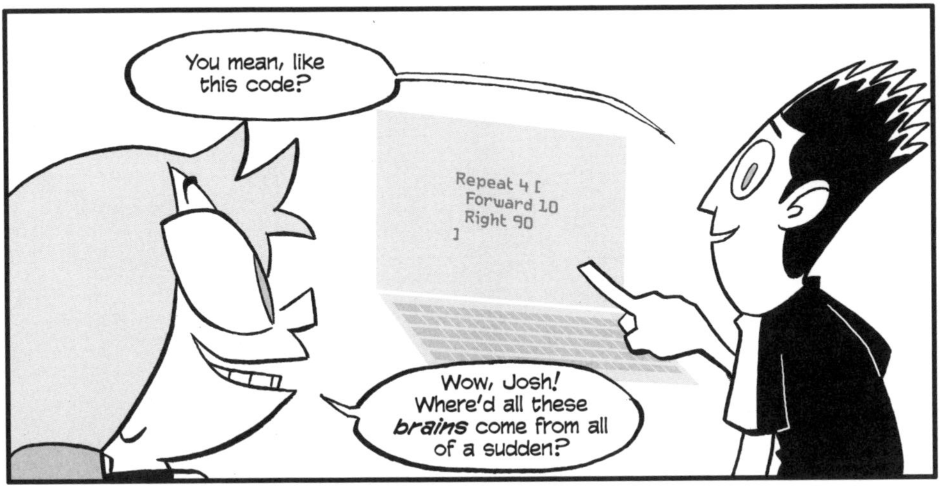
You mean, like this code?
Repeat 4 [
Forward 10
Right 90
]
Wow, Josh! Where'd all these *brains* come from all of a sudden?

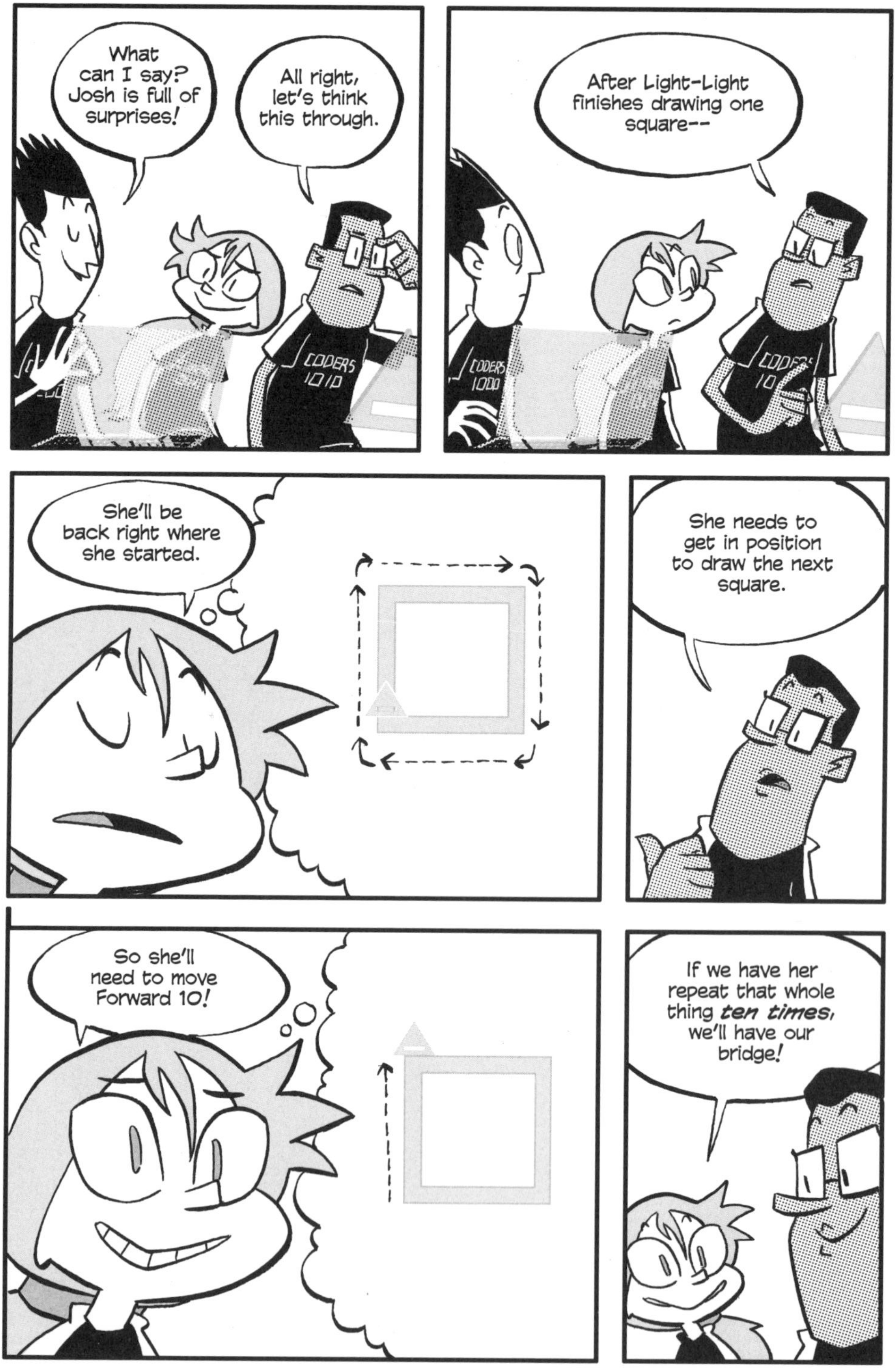
What can I say? Josh is full of surprises!
All right, let's think this through.
After Light-Light finishes drawing one square--
She'll be back right where she started.
She needs to get in position to draw the next square.
So she'll need to move Forward 10!
If we have her repeat that whole thing ***ten times***, we'll have our bridge!

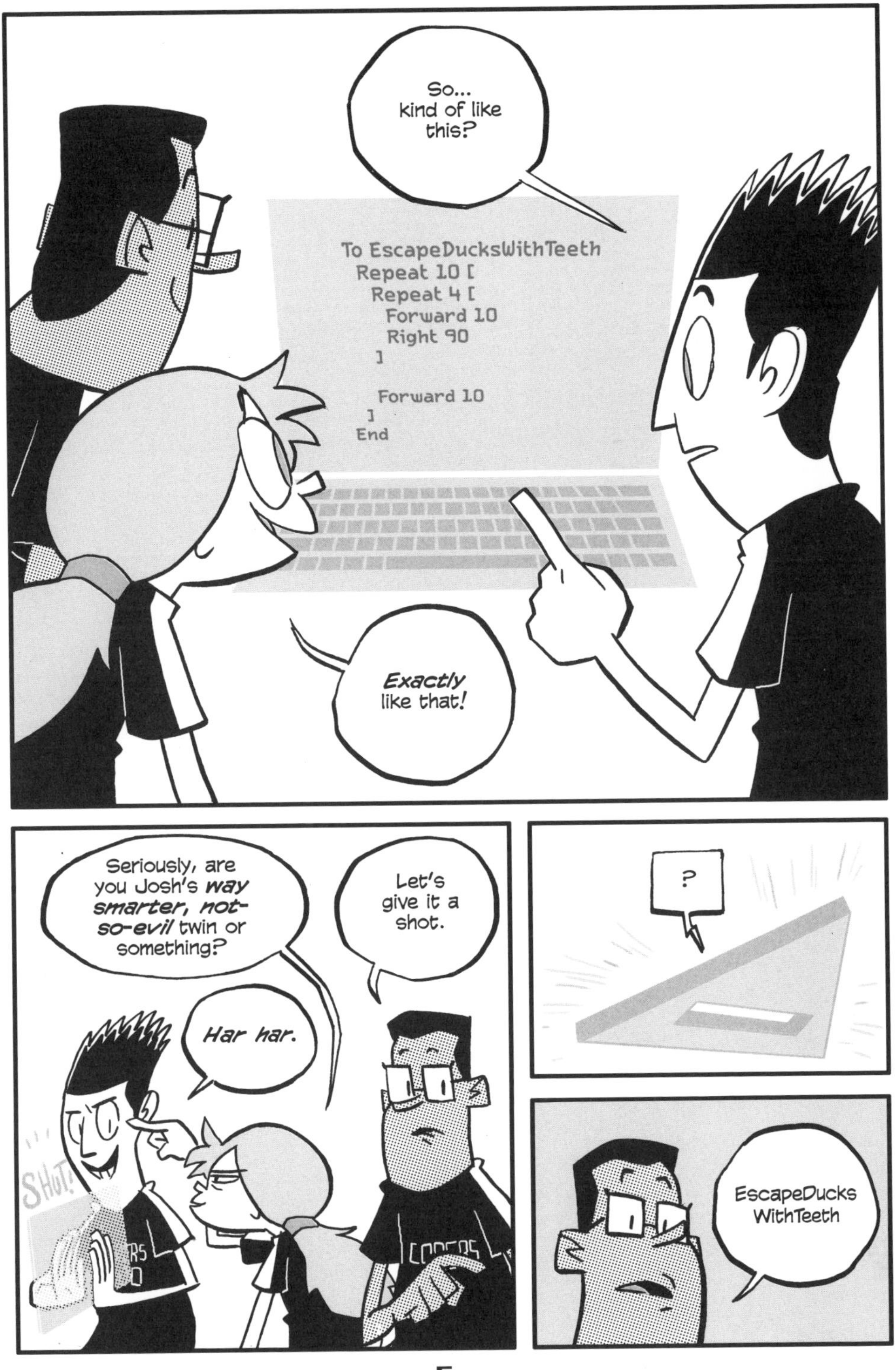
So... kind of like this?
To EscapeDucksWithTeeth
Repeat 10 [
Repeat 4 [
Forward 10
Right 90
]
Forward 10
]
End
Exactly like that!
Seriously, are you Josh's ***way smarter, not-so-evil*** twin or something?
Har har.
Let's give it a shot.
?
EscapeDucks WithTeeth

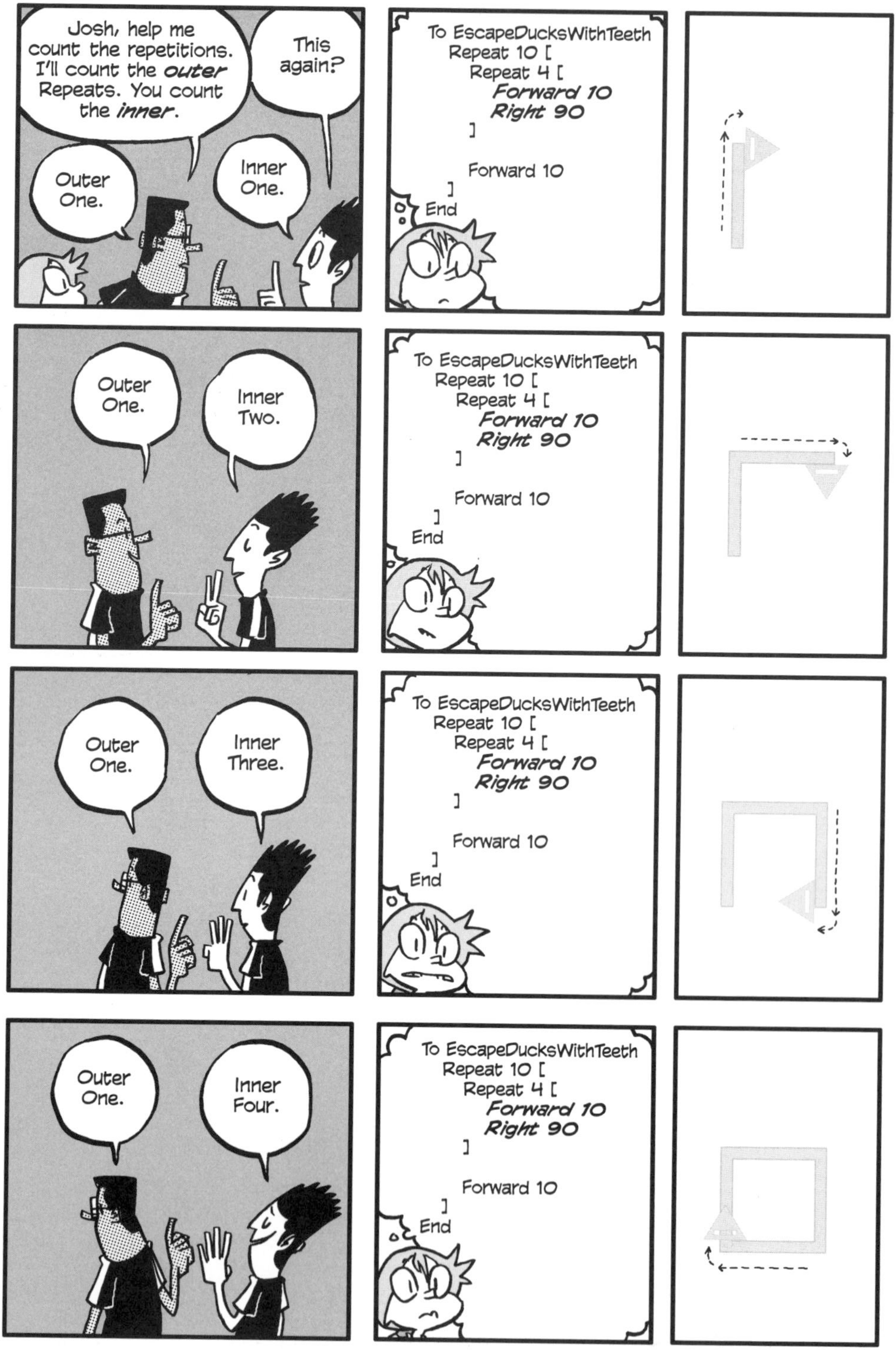
Josh, help me count the repetitions. I'll count the *outer* Repeats. You count the *inner*.
This again?
Outer One.
Inner One.
To EscapeDucksWithTeeth
Repeat 10 [
Repeat 4 [
Forward 10
Right 90
]
Forward 10
]
End
Outer One.
Inner Two.
To EscapeDucksWithTeeth
Repeat 10 [
Repeat 4 [
Forward 10
Right 90
]
Forward 10
]
End
Outer One.
Inner Three.
To EscapeDucksWithTeeth
Repeat 10 [
Repeat 4 [
Forward 10
Right 90
]
Forward 10
]
End
Outer One.
Inner Four.
To EscapeDucksWithTeeth
Repeat 10 [
Repeat 4 [
Forward 10
Right 90
]
Forward 10
]
End

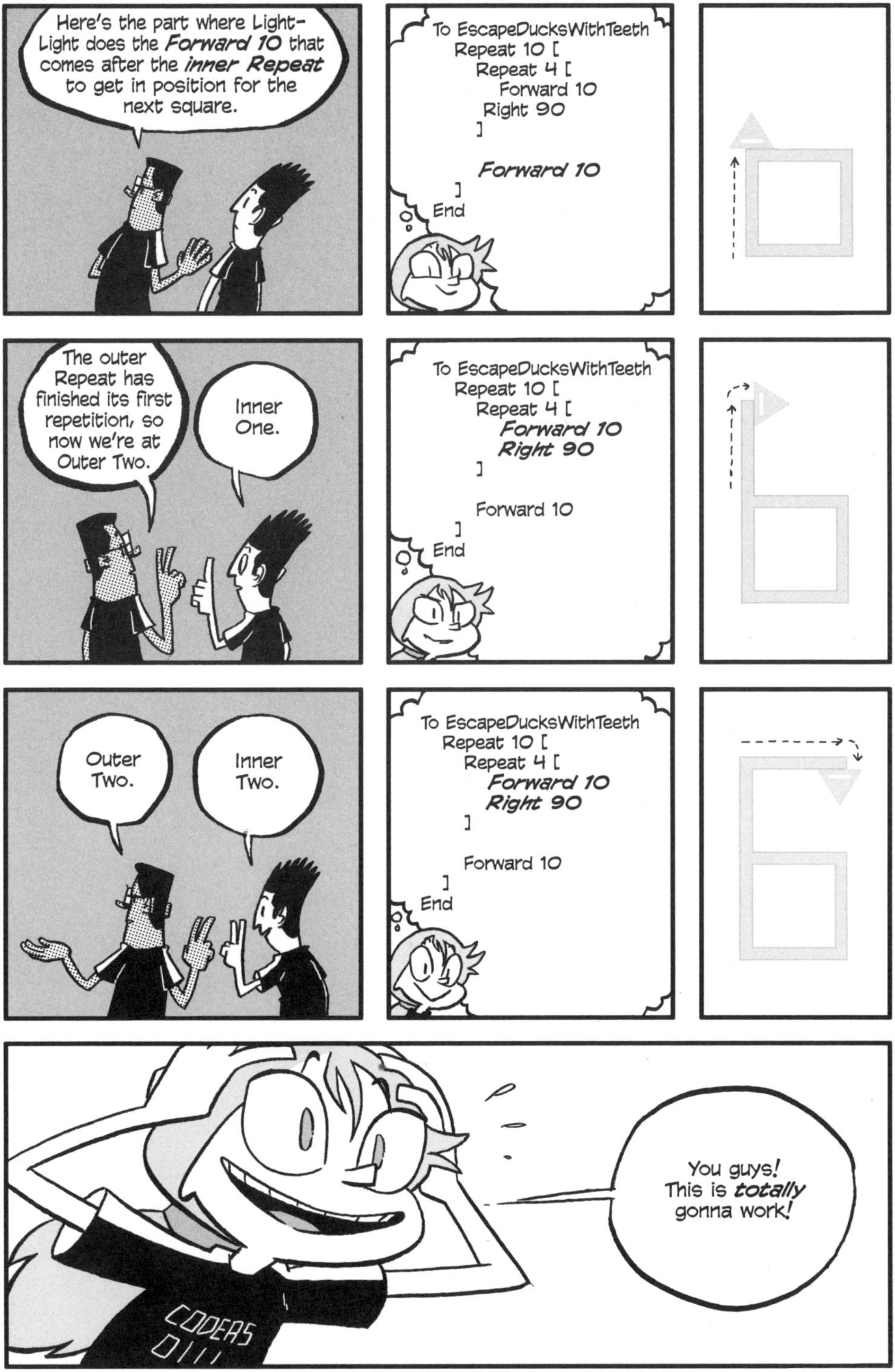

Here's the part where Light-Light does the Forward 10 that comes after the inner Repeat to get in position for the next square.
To EscapeDucksWithTeeth
Repeat 10 [
Repeat 4 [
Forward 10
Right 90
]
Forward 10
]
End
The outer Repeat has finished its first repetition, so now we're at Outer Two.
Inner One.
To EscapeDucksWithTeeth
Repeat 10 [
Repeat 4 [
Forward 10
Right 90
]
Forward 10
]
End
Outer Two.
Inner Two.
To EscapeDucksWithTeeth
Repeat 10 [
Repeat 4 [
Forward 10
Right 90
]
Forward 10
]
End
You guys! This is totally gonna work!

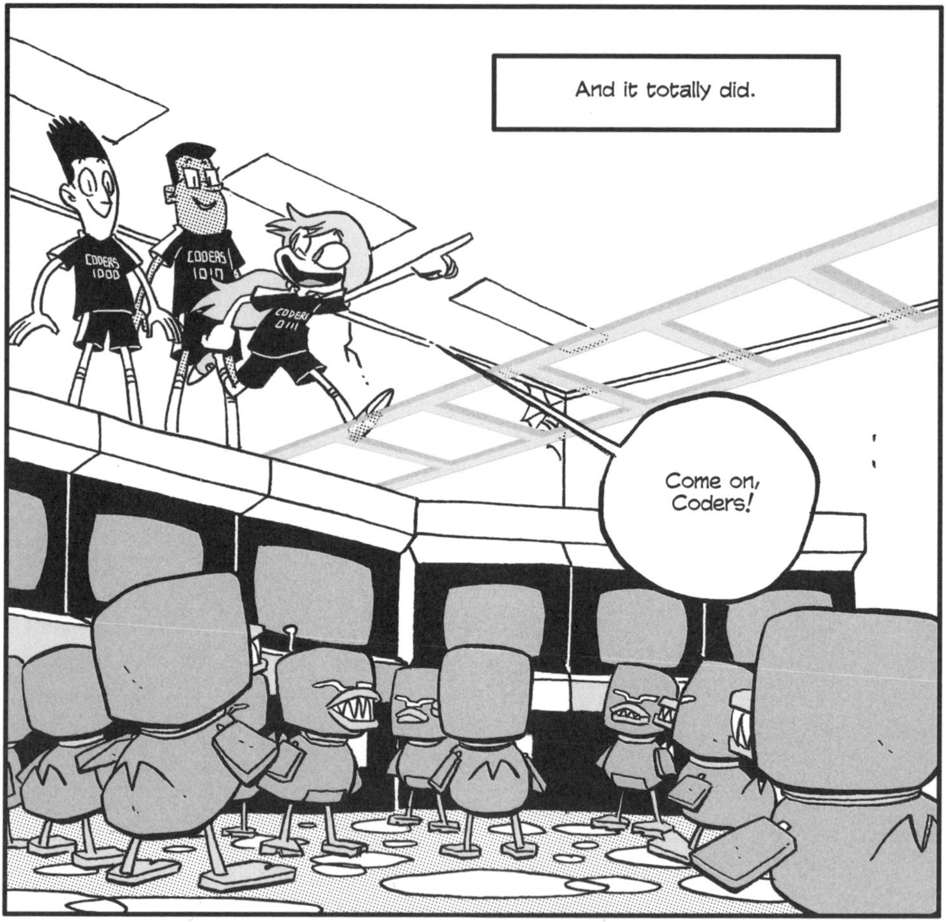
And it totally did.
Come on, Coders!
CODERS 1000
CODERS 1010
CODERS 0111

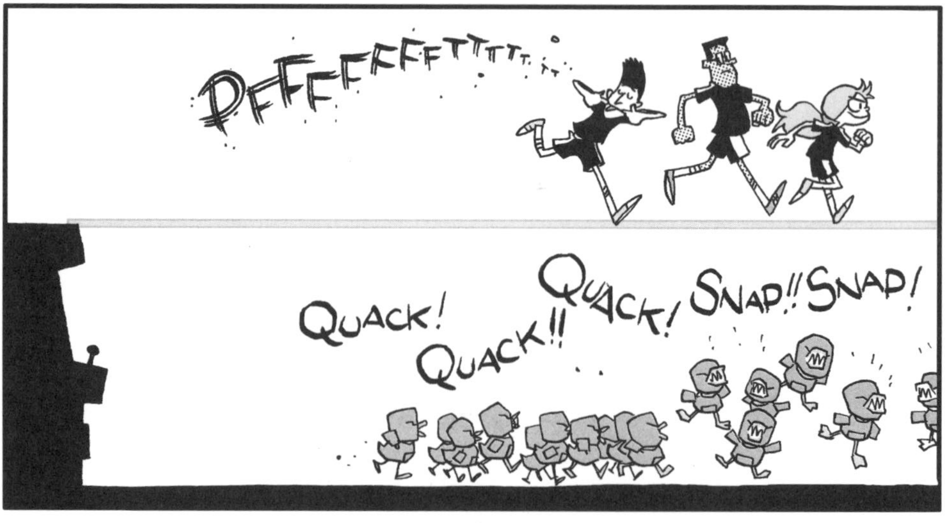
PFFFFFFFTTTTT
QUACK!
QUACK!!
QUACK!
SNAP!! SNAP!

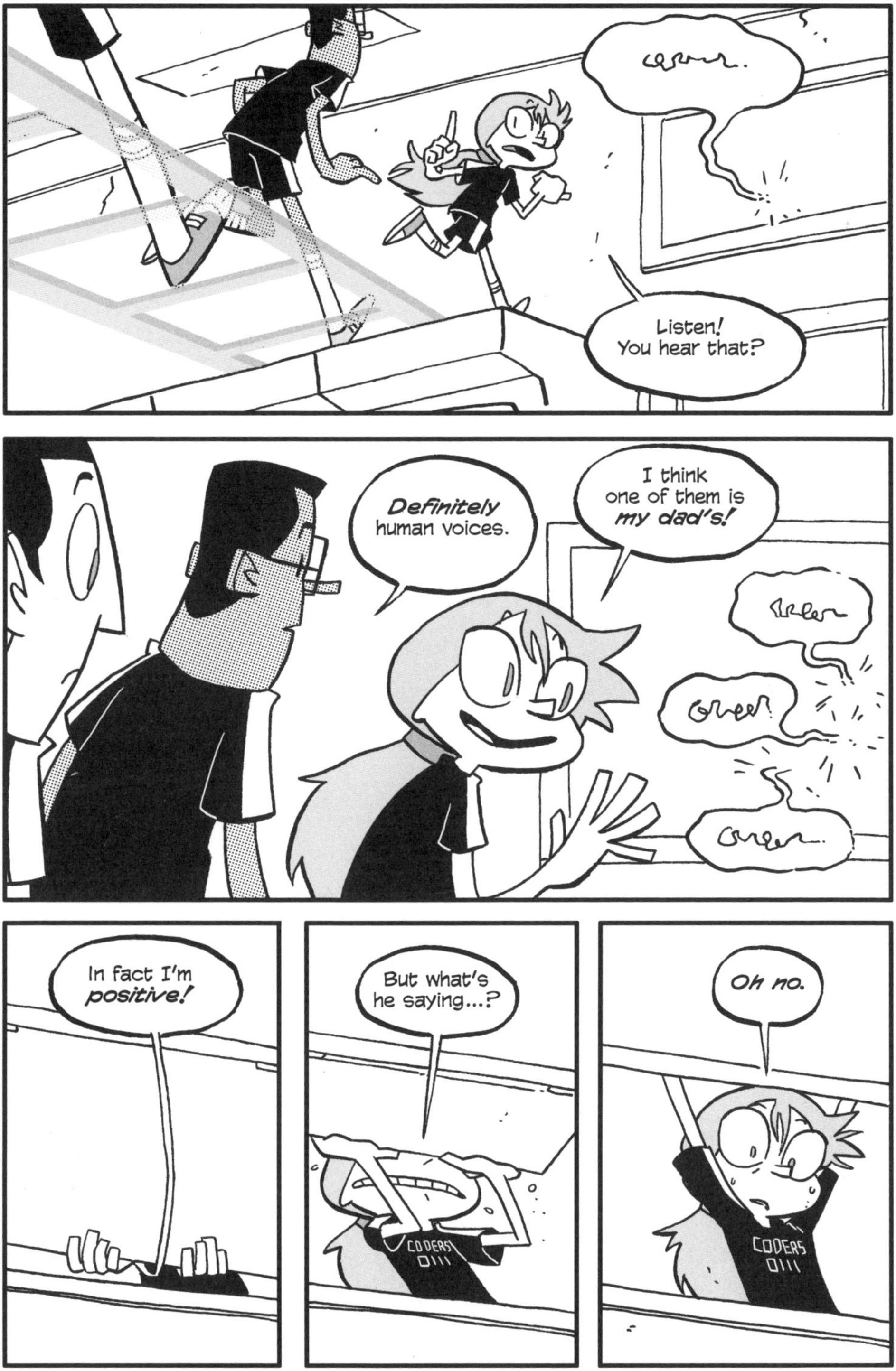
Listen!
You hear that?
Definitely
human voices.
I think
one of them is
my dad's!
In fact I'm
positive!
But what's
he saying...?
Oh no.
CODERS
0111
CODERS
0111

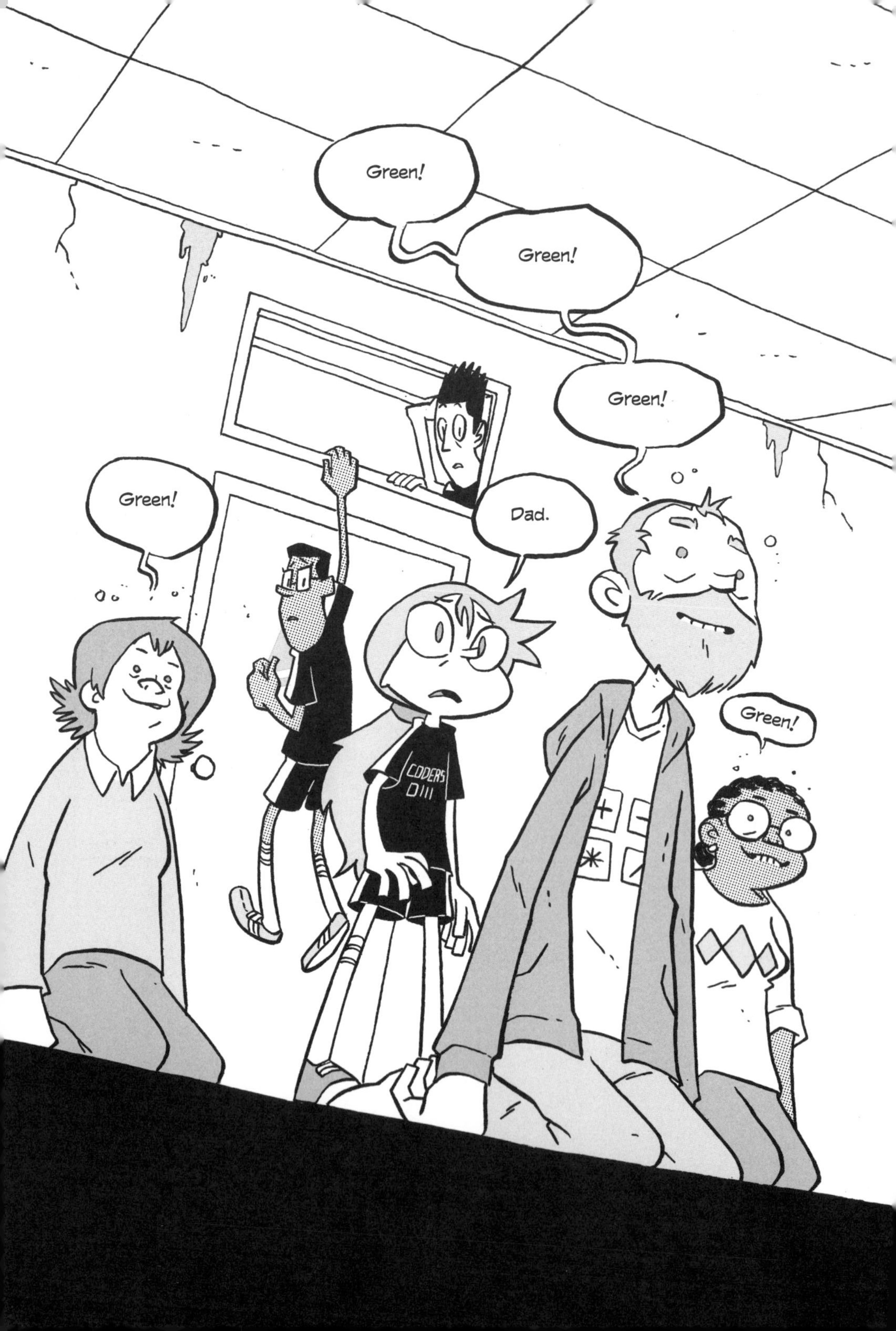
Green!
Green!
Green!
Green!
Dad.
Green!
CODERS
D III

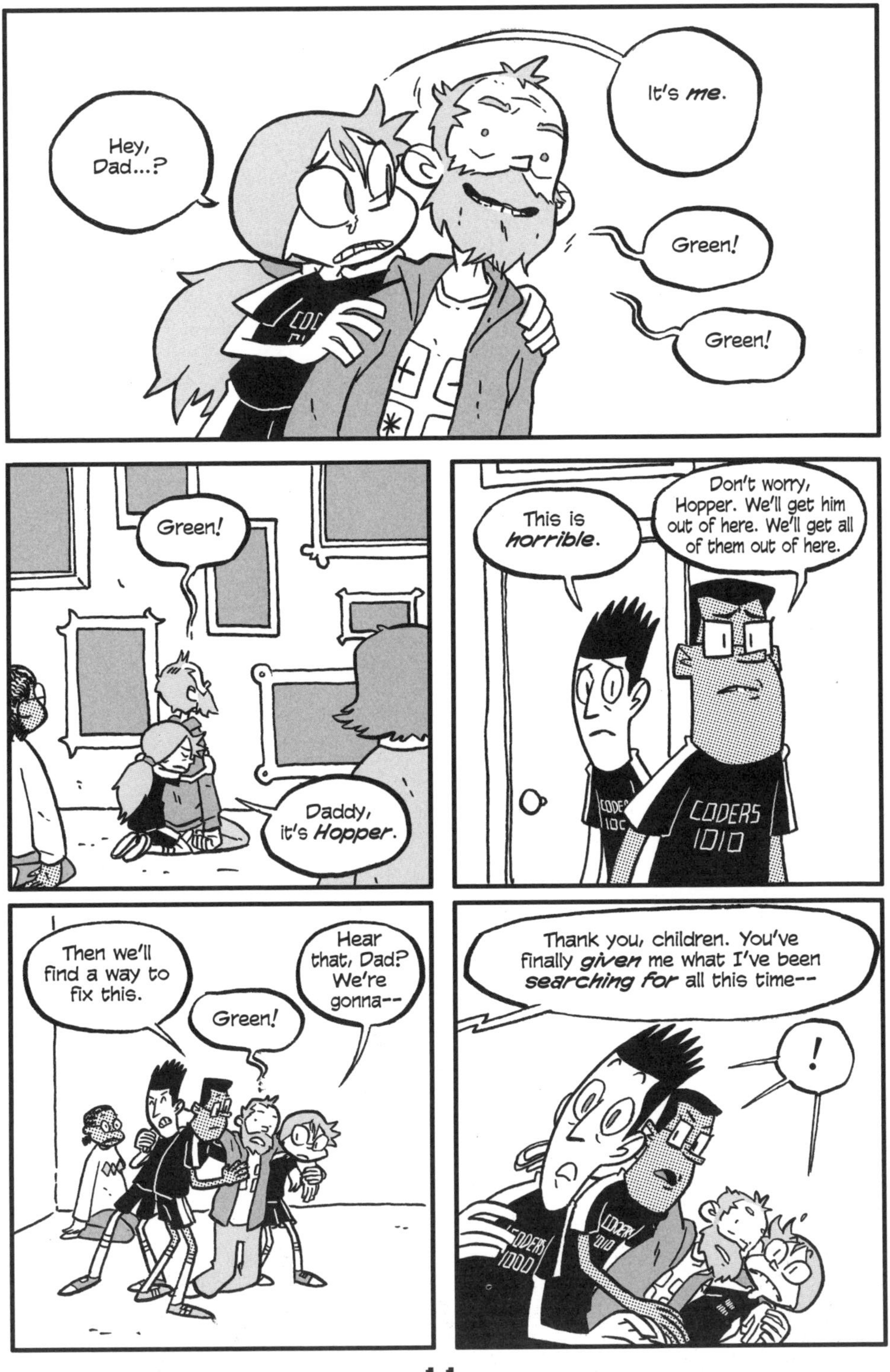
Hey, Dad...?
It's *me*.
Green!
Green!
CODERS
Green!
Daddy, it's *Hopper*.
This is *horrible*.
Don't worry, Hopper. We'll get him out of here. We'll get all of them out of here.
CODERS 1010
Then we'll find a way to fix this.
Green!
Hear that, Dad? We're gonna--
Thank you, children. You've finally *given* me what I've been *searching for* all this time--
!
CODERS 1010

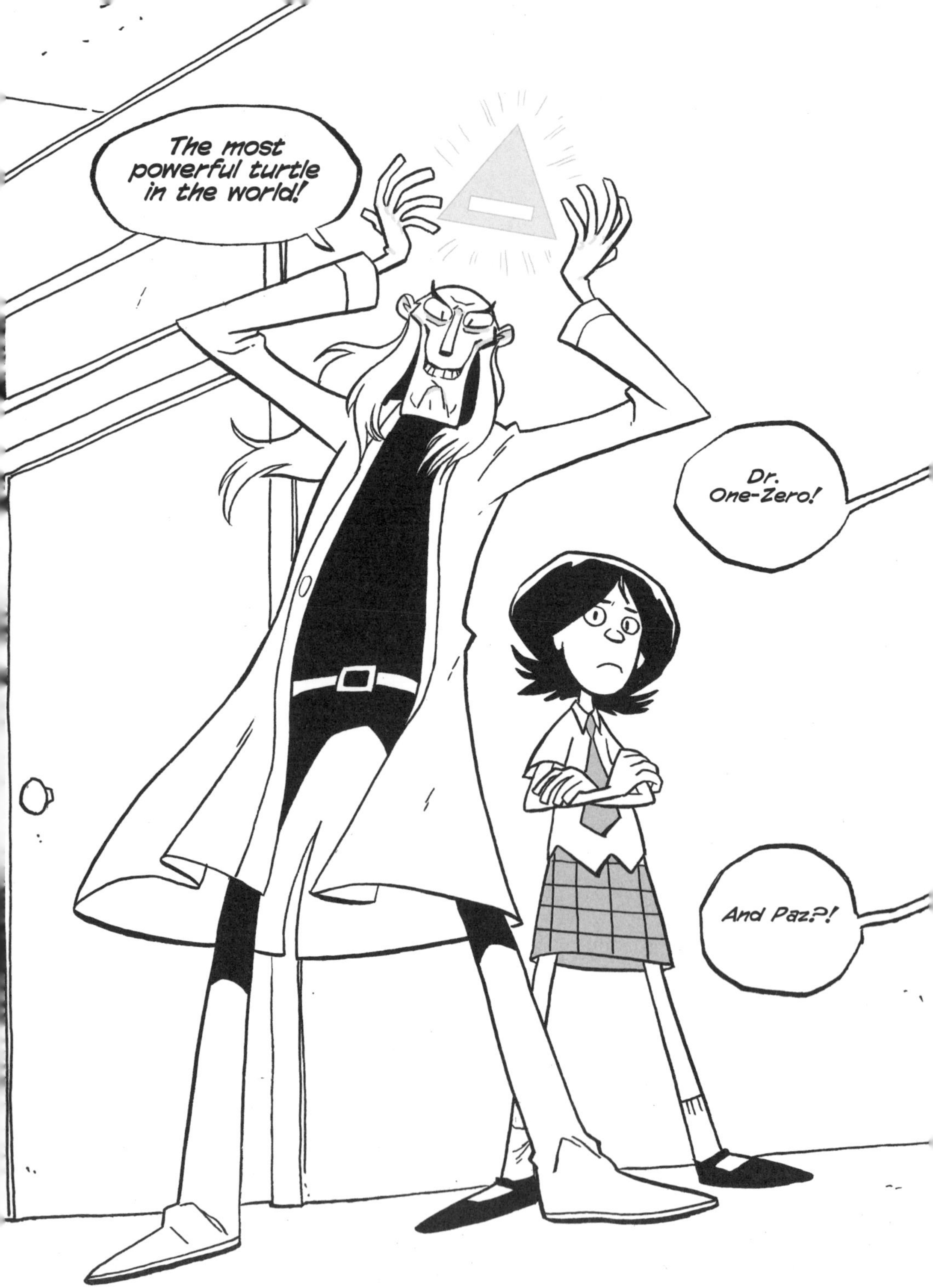
The most powerful turtle in the world!
Dr. One-Zero!
And Paz?!

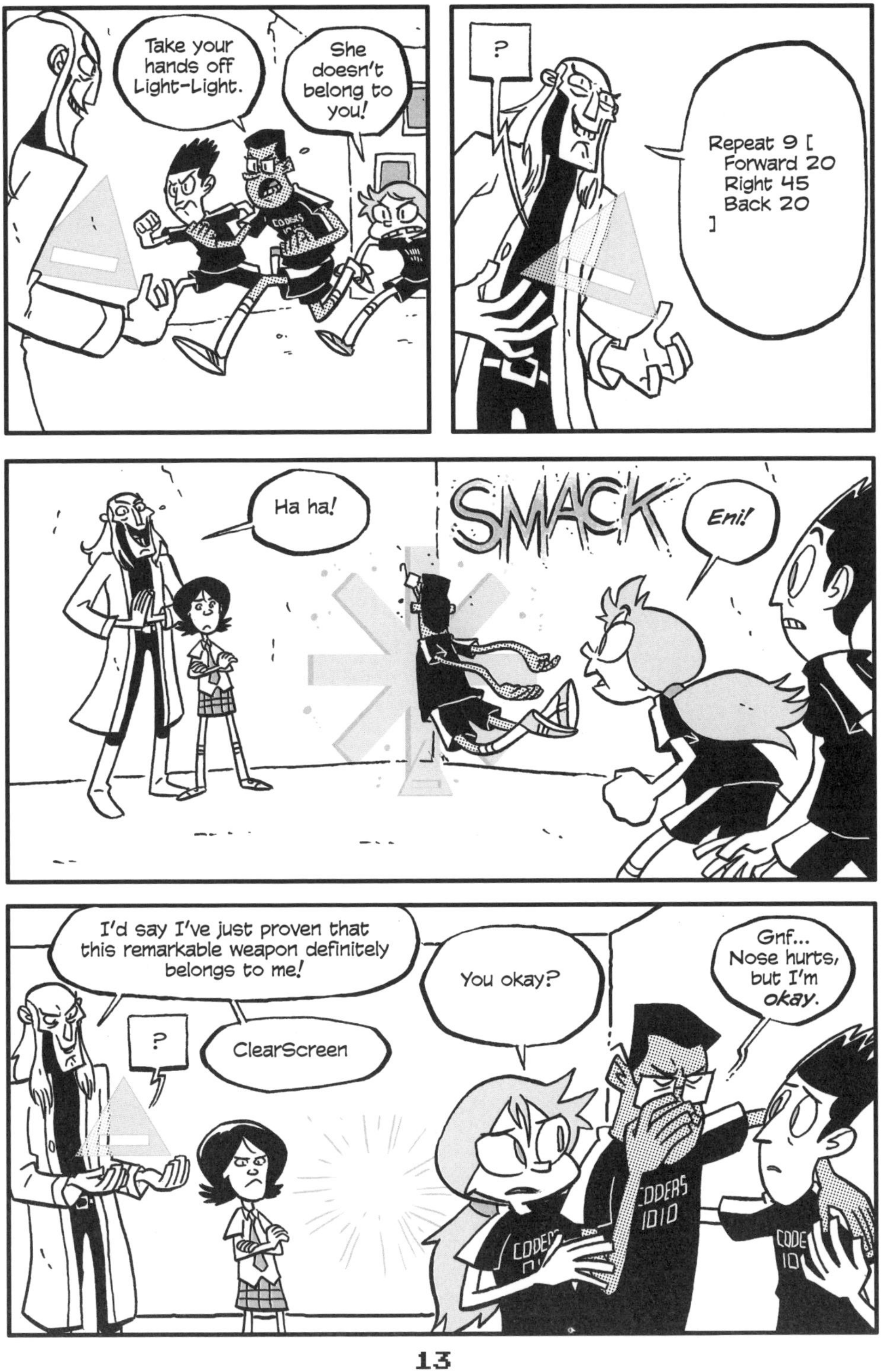
Take your hands off Light-Light.
She doesn't belong to you!
?
Repeat 9 [
Forward 20
Right 45
Back 20
]
Ha ha!
SMACK
Eni!
I'd say I've just proven that this remarkable weapon definitely belongs to me!
?
ClearScreen
You okay?
Gnf... Nose hurts, but I'm *okay*.

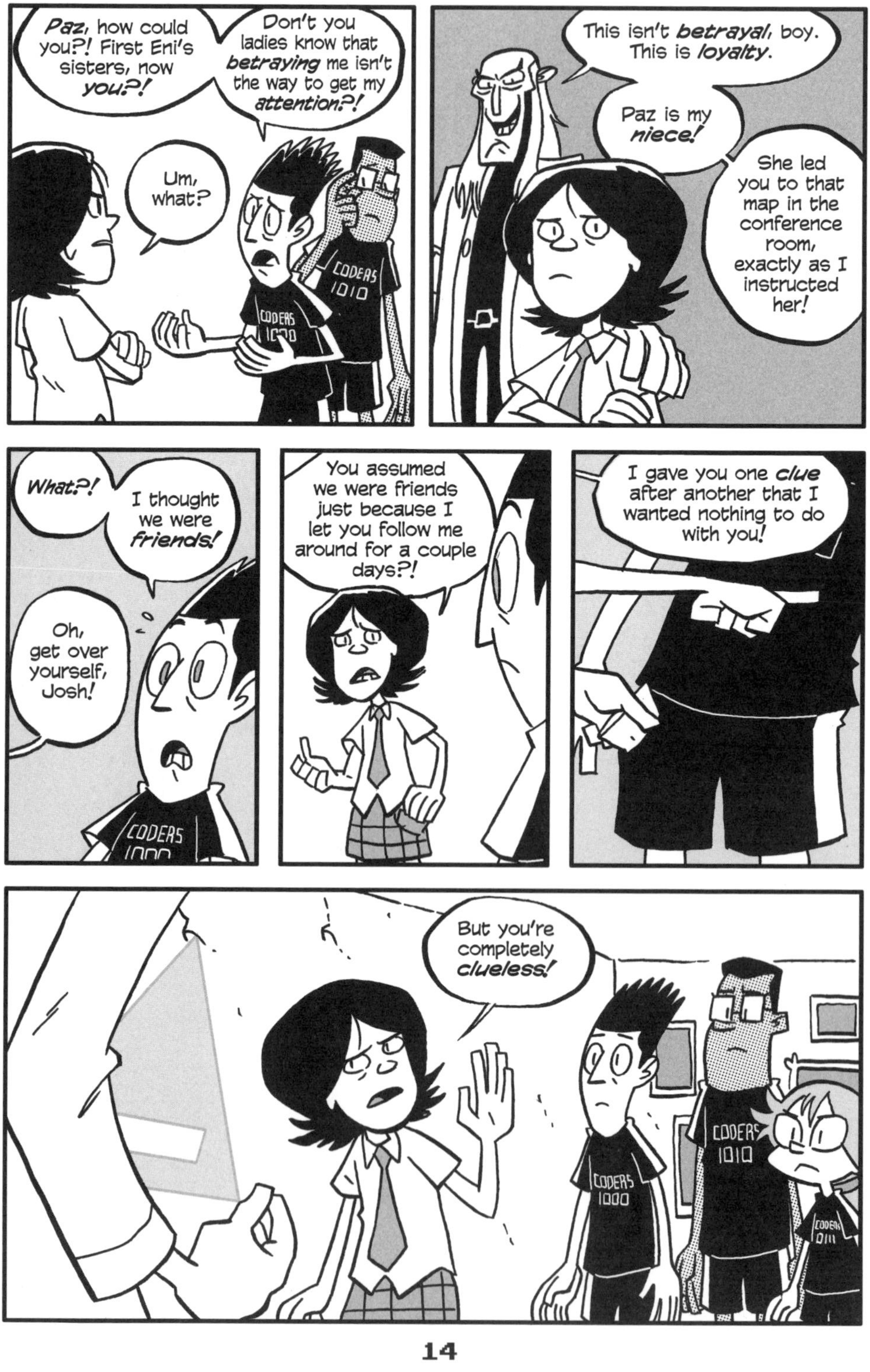
Paz, how could you?! First Eni's sisters, now you?!
Don't you ladies know that betraying me isn't the way to get my attention?!
Um, what?
This isn't betrayal, boy. This is loyalty.
Paz is my niece!
She led you to that map in the conference room, exactly as I instructed her!
What?!
I thought we were friends!
Oh, get over yourself, Josh!
You assumed we were friends just because I let you follow me around for a couple days?!
I gave you one clue after another that I wanted nothing to do with you!
But you're completely clueless!

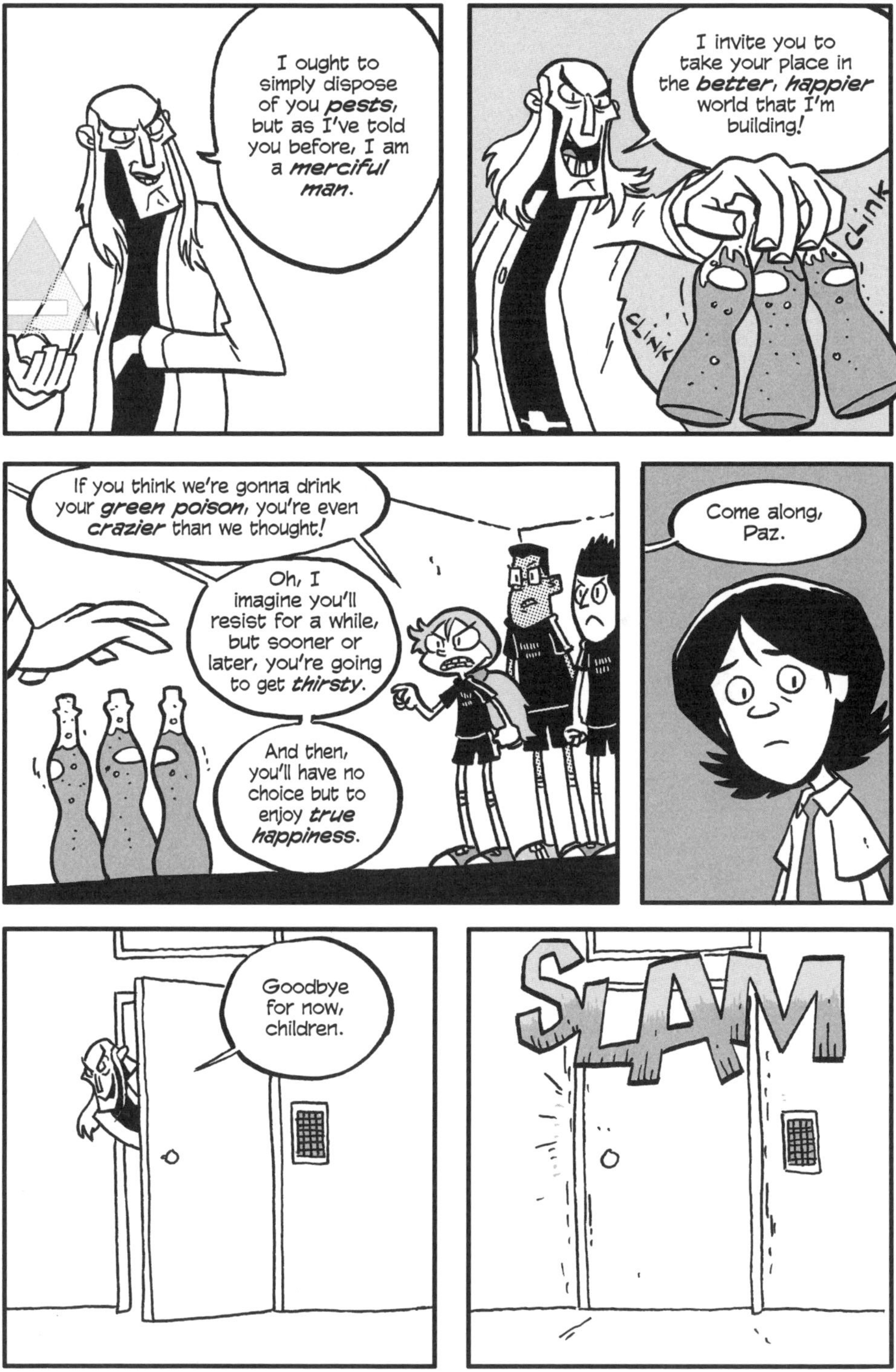
I ought to simply dispose of you *pests*, but as I've told you before, I am a *merciful man*.
I invite you to take your place in the *better*, *happier* world that I'm building!
CLINK
CLINK
If you think we're gonna drink your *green poison*, you're even *crazier* than we thought!
Oh, I imagine you'll resist for a while, but sooner or later, you're going to get *thirsty*.
And then, you'll have no choice but to enjoy *true happiness*.
Come along, Paz.
Goodbye for now, children.
SLAM

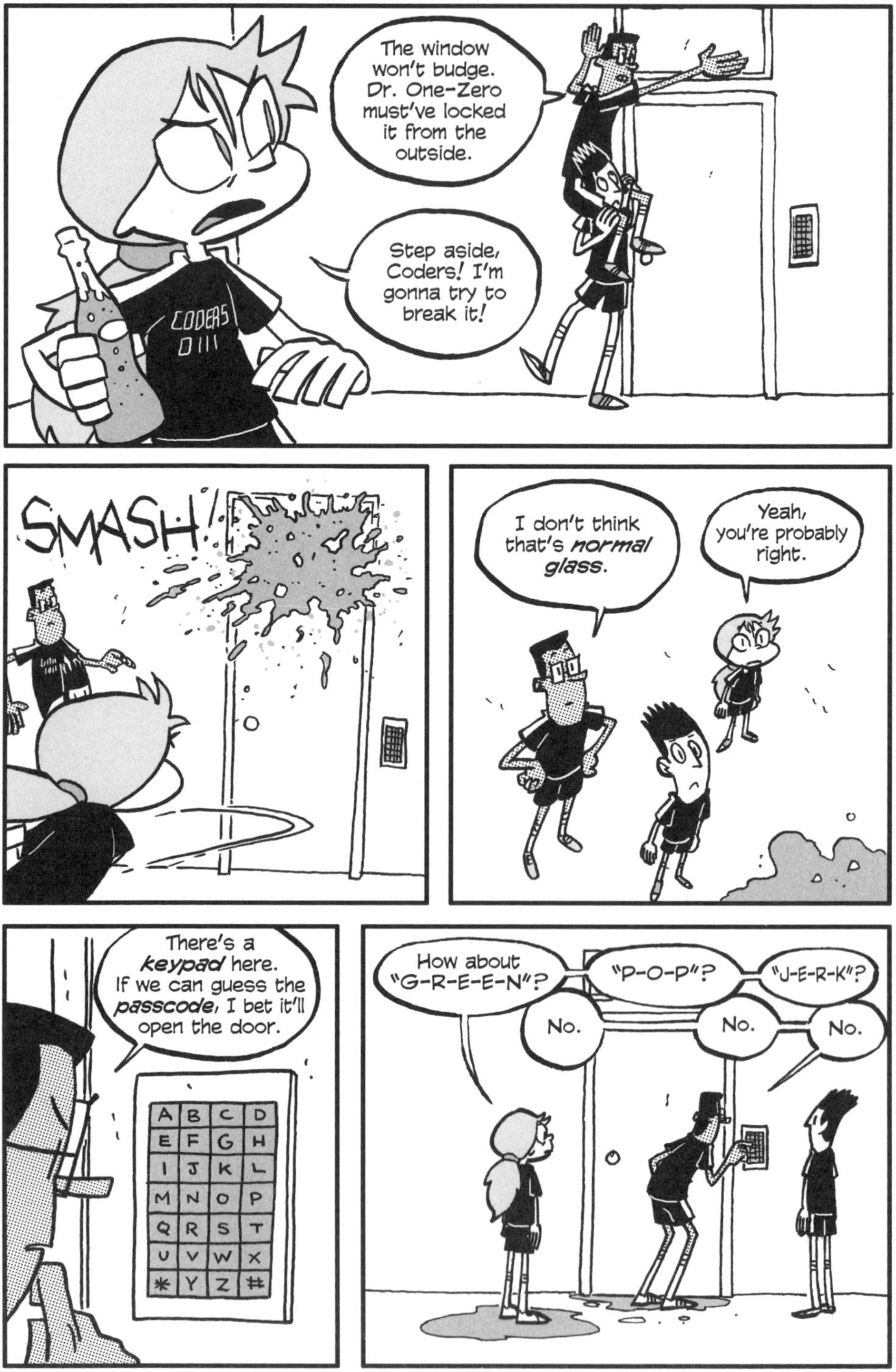

The window won't budge. Dr. One-Zero must've locked it from the outside.
Step aside, Coders! I'm gonna try to break it!
CODERS 0111
SMASH!
I don't think that's *normal glass*.
Yeah, you're probably right.
There's a *keypad* here. If we can guess the *passcode*, I bet it'll open the door.
A B C D E F G H I J K L M N O P Q R S T U V W X * Y Z #
How about "G-R-E-E-N"?
No.
"P-O-P"?
No.
"J-E-R-K"?
No.

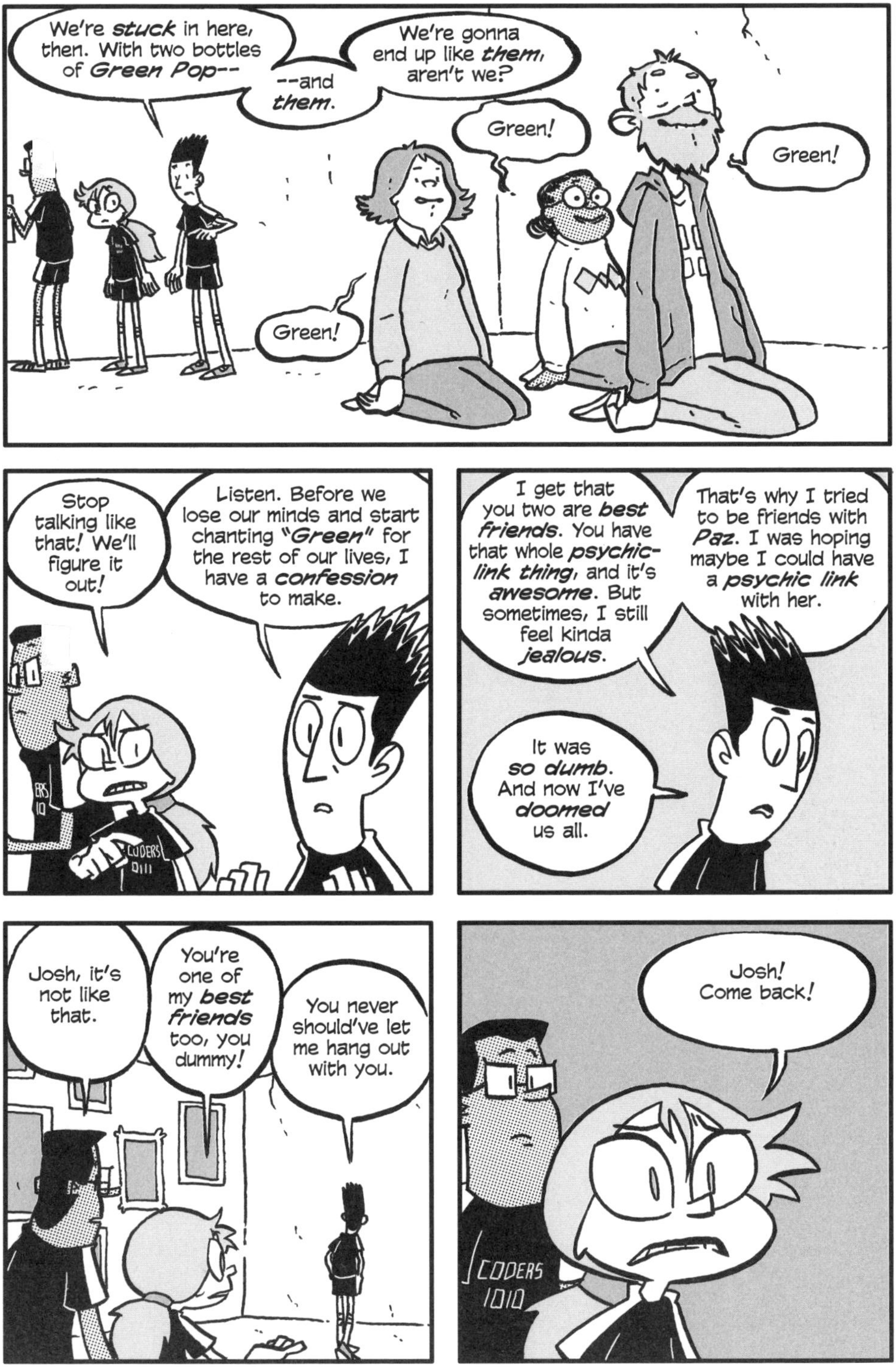
We're *stuck* in here, then. With two bottles of *Green Pop*--
--and *them*.
We're gonna end up like *them*, aren't we?
Green!
Green!
Green!
Stop talking like that! We'll figure it out!
Listen. Before we lose our minds and start chanting "*Green*" for the rest of our lives, I have a *confession* to make.
I get that you two are *best friends*. You have that whole *psychic-link thing*, and it's *awesome*. But sometimes, I still feel kinda *jealous*.
That's why I tried to be friends with *Paz*. I was hoping maybe I could have a *psychic link* with her.
It was *so dumb*. And now I've *doomed* us all.
Josh, it's not like that.
You're one of my *best friends* too, you dummy!
You never should've let me hang out with you.
Josh! Come back!

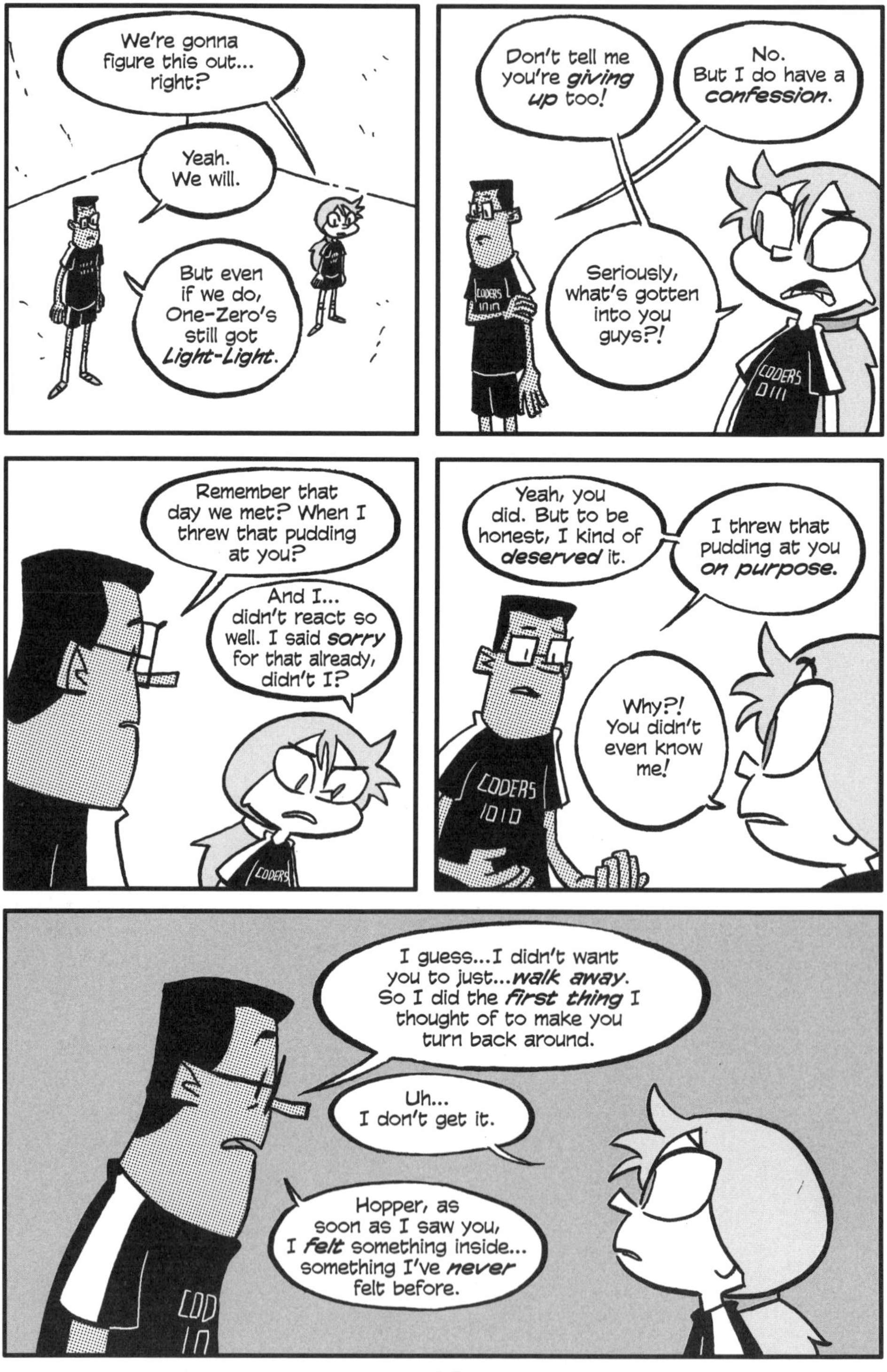
We're gonna figure this out... right?
Yeah. We will.
But even if we do, One-Zero's still got *Light-Light*.
Don't tell me you're *giving up* too!
No. But I do have a *confession*.
Seriously, what's gotten into you guys?!
CODERS 1010
CODERS 1011
Remember that day we met? When I threw that pudding at you?
And I... didn't react so well. I said *sorry* for that already, didn't I?
CODERS
Yeah, you did. But to be honest, I kind of *deserved* it.
I threw that pudding at you *on purpose.*
Why?! You didn't even know me!
CODERS 1010
I guess...I didn't want you to just...*walk away*. So I did the *first thing* I thought of to make you turn back around.
Uh... I don't get it.
Hopper, as soon as I saw you, I *felt* something inside... something I've *never* felt before.

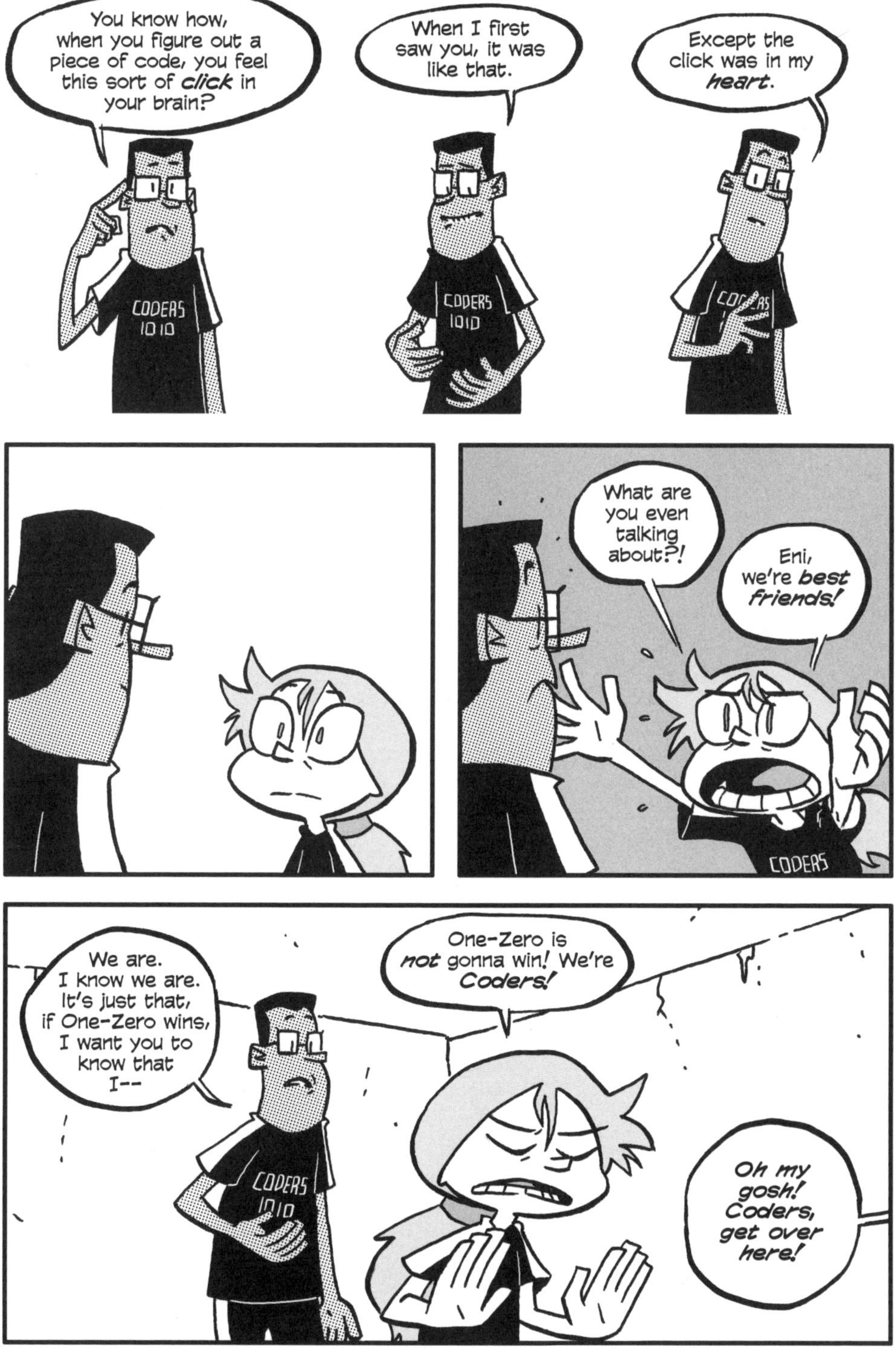
You know how, when you figure out a piece of code, you feel this sort of *click* in your brain?
When I first saw you, it was like that.
Except the click was in my *heart*.
CODERS 1010
CODERS 1010
CODERS
What are you even talking about?!
Eni, we're *best friends!*
CODERS
We are. I know we are. It's just that, if One-Zero wins, I want you to know that I--
One-Zero is *not* gonna win! We're *Coders!*
CODERS 1010
Oh my gosh! Coders, get over here!

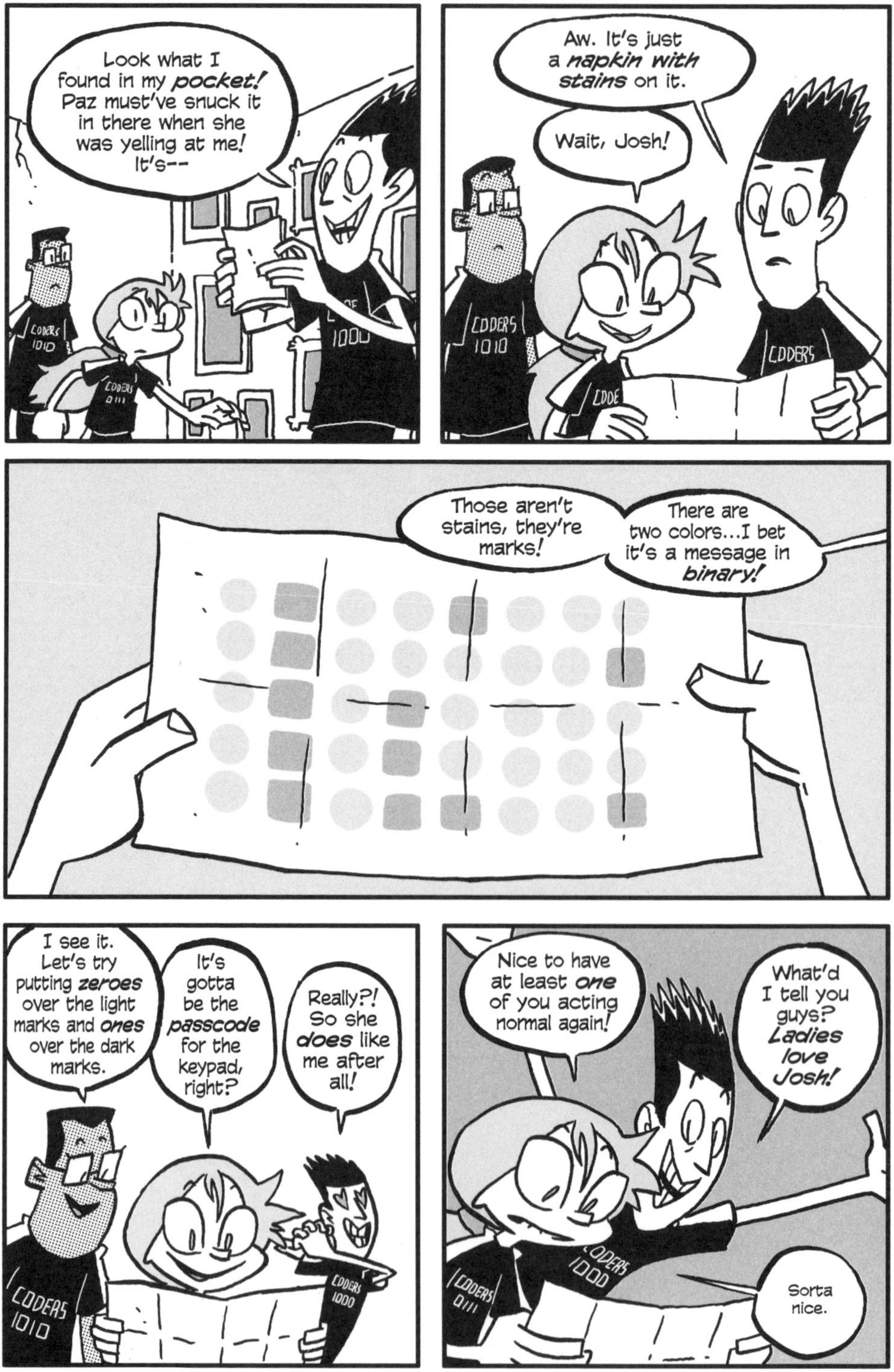
Look what I found in my pocket! Paz must've snuck it in there when she was yelling at me! It's--
CODERS 1010
CODERS 0111
CODE 1000
Aw. It's just a napkin with stains on it.
Wait, Josh!
CODERS 1010
CODE
CODERS
Those aren't stains, they're marks!
There are two colors...I bet it's a message in binary!
I see it. Let's try putting zeroes over the light marks and ones over the dark marks.
It's gotta be the passcode for the keypad, right?
Really?! So she does like me after all!
CODERS 1010
CODERS 1000
Nice to have at least one of you acting normal again!
What'd I tell you guys? Ladies love Josh!
CODERS 1000
CODERS 0111
Sorta nice.

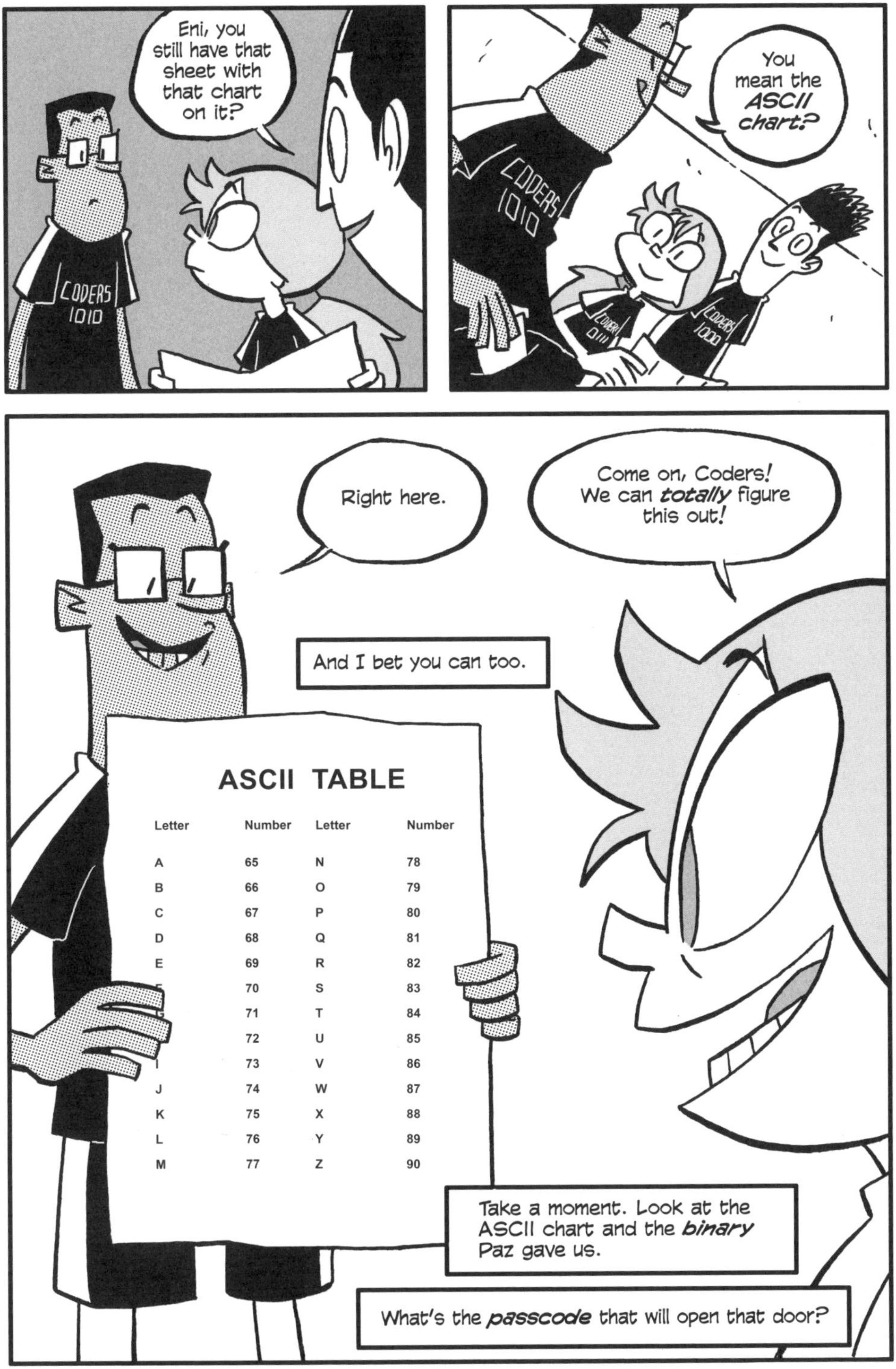
Eni, you still have that sheet with that chart on it?
CODERS 1010
You mean the *ASCII chart?*
CODERS 1010
CODERS 0111
CODERS 1000
Right here.
Come on, Coders! We can *totally* figure this out!
And I bet you can too.
ASCII TABLE
Letter Number Letter Number
A 65 N 78
B 66 O 79
C 67 P 80
D 68 Q 81
E 69 R 82
70 S 83
71 T 84
72 U 85
73 V 86
J 74 W 87
K 75 X 88
L 76 Y 89
M 77 Z 90
Take a moment. Look at the ASCII chart and the *binary* Paz gave us.
What's the *passcode* that will open that door?

Chapter

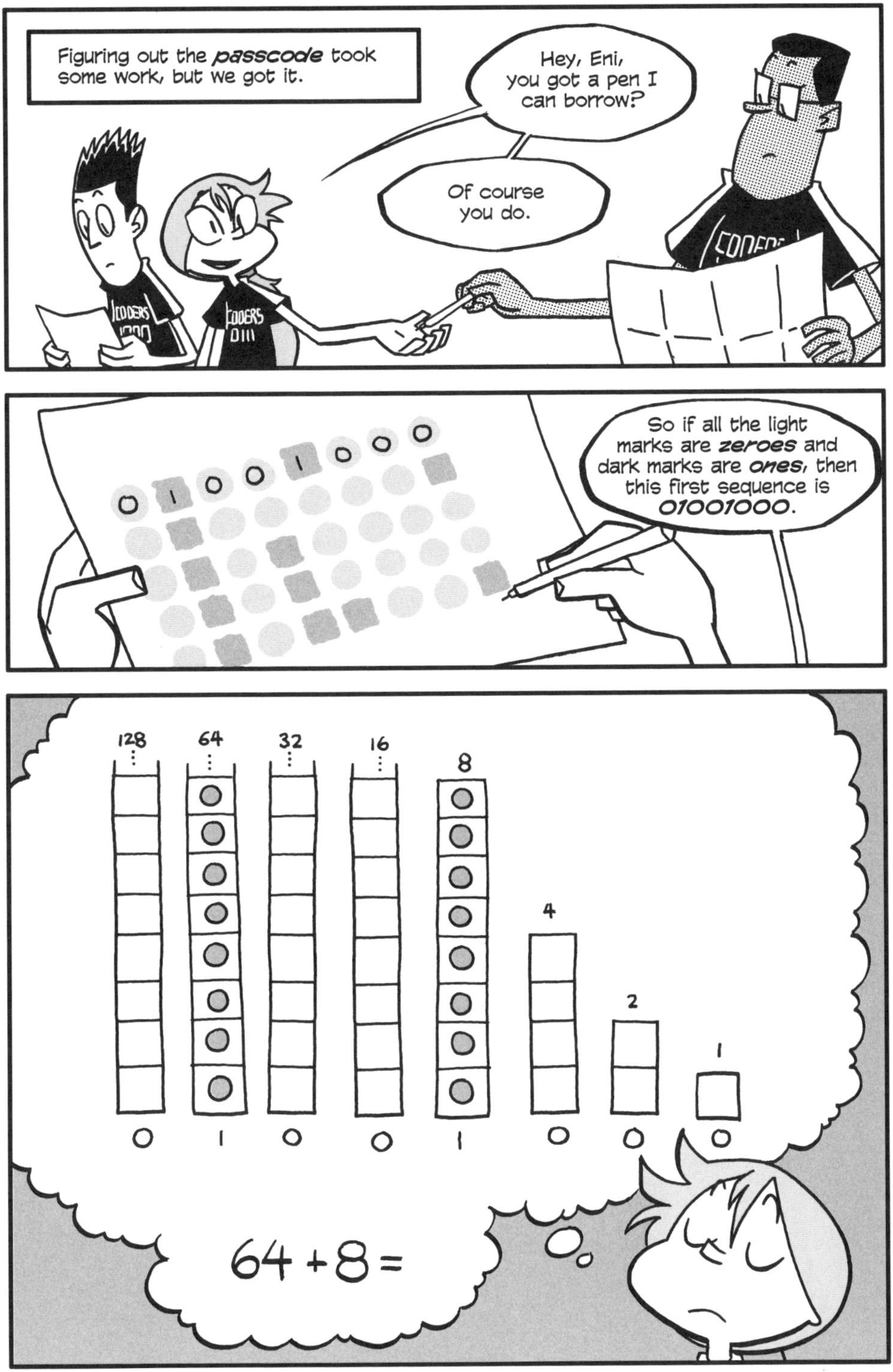
Figuring out the ***passcode*** took some work, but we got it.
Hey, Eni, you got a pen I can borrow?
Of course you do.
CODERS 1000
CODERS 0111
0 1 0 0 1 0 0 0
So if all the light marks are ***zeroes*** and dark marks are ***ones***, then this first sequence is ***01001000***.
128
64
32
16
8
4
2
1
0 1 0 0 1 0 0 0
64 + 8 =

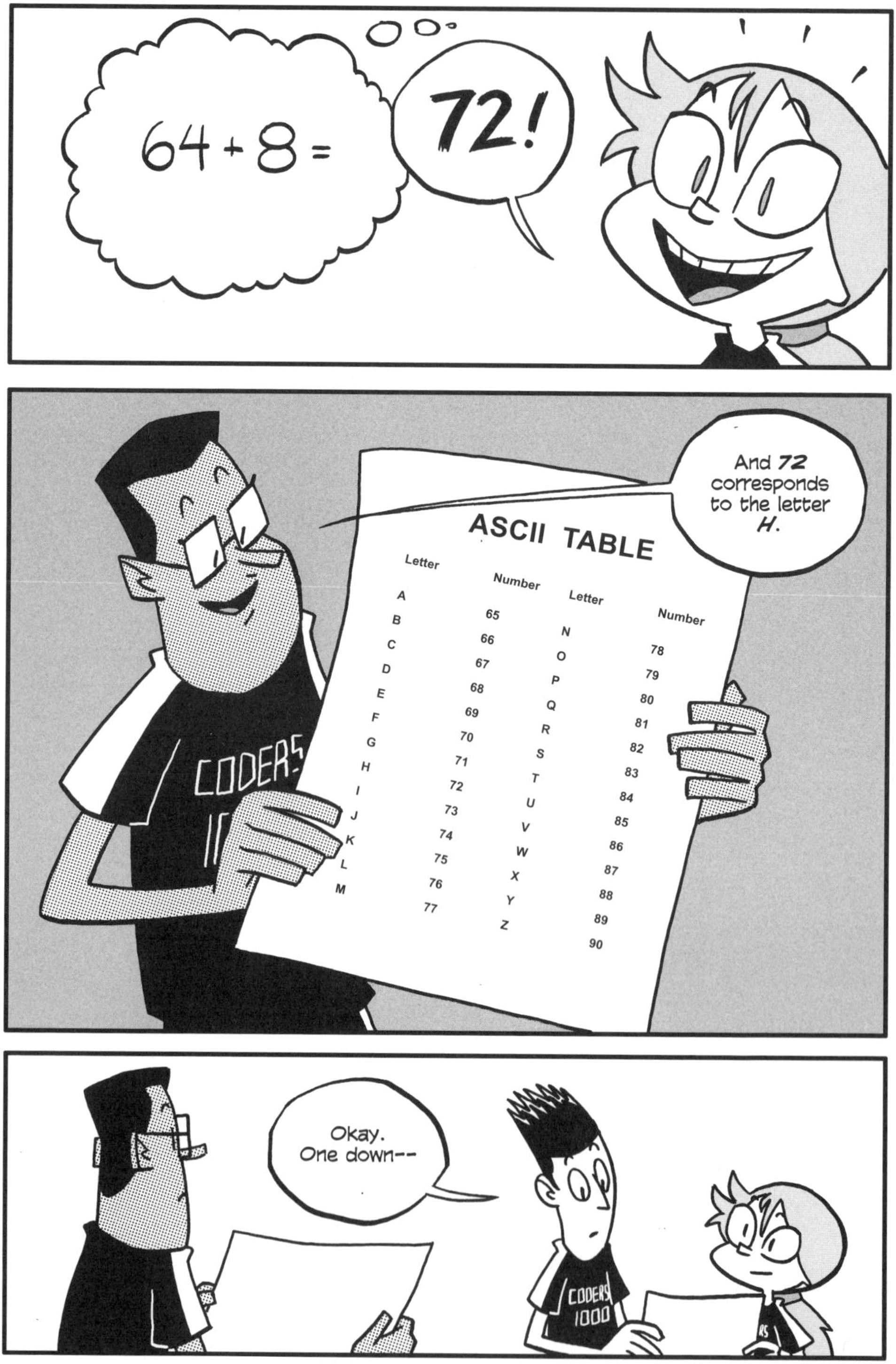
64+8=
72!
ASCII TABLE
Letter Number Letter Number
A 65 N 78
B 66 O 79
C 67 P 80
D 68 Q 81
E 69 R 82
F 70 S 83
G 71 T 84
H 72 U 85
I 73 V 86
J 74 W 87
K 75 X 88
L 76 Y 89
M 77 Z 90
And 72 corresponds to the letter H.
CODERS
Okay. One down--
CODERS 1000

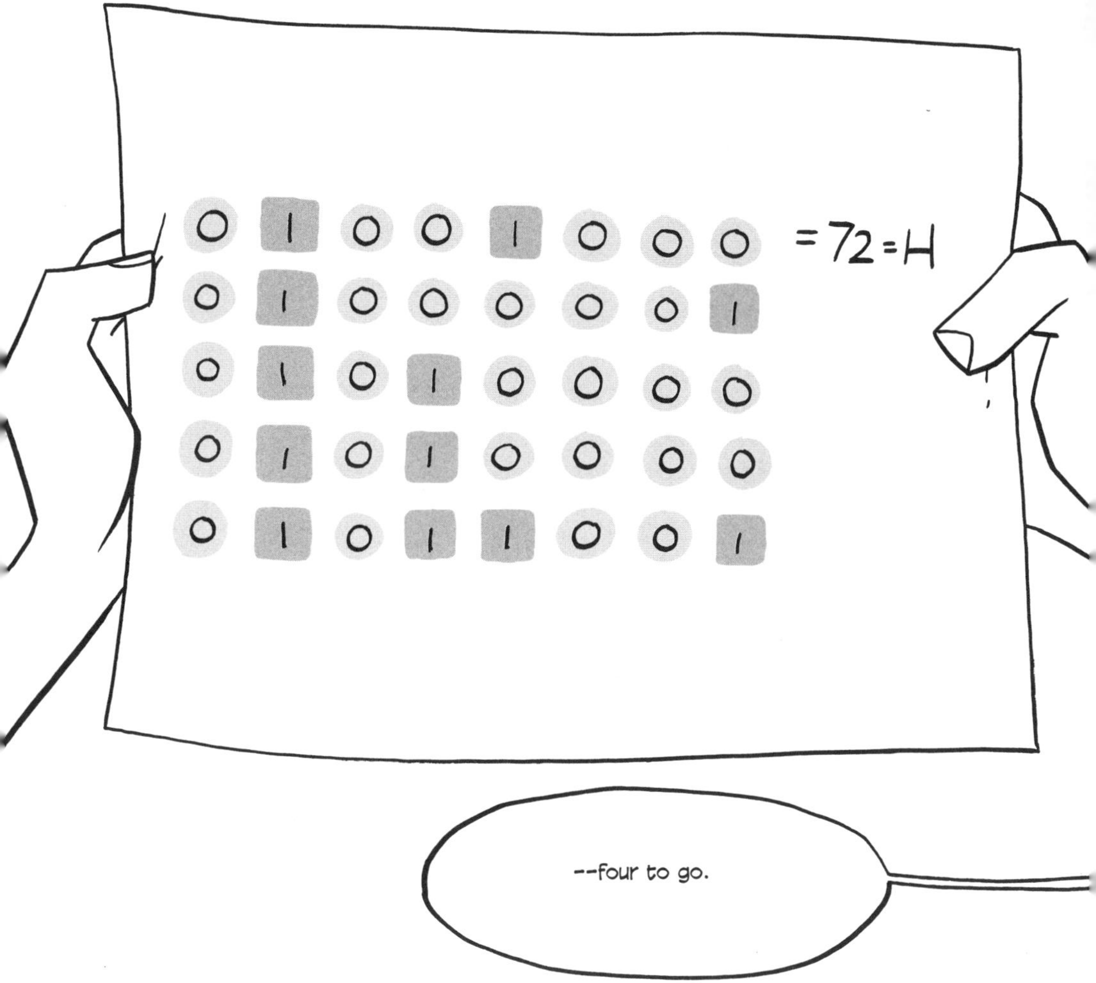
0 1 0 0 1 0 0 0 =72=H
0 1 0 0 0 0 0 1
0 1 0 1 0 0 0 0
0 1 0 1 0 0 0 0
0 1 0 1 1 0 0 1
--four to go.

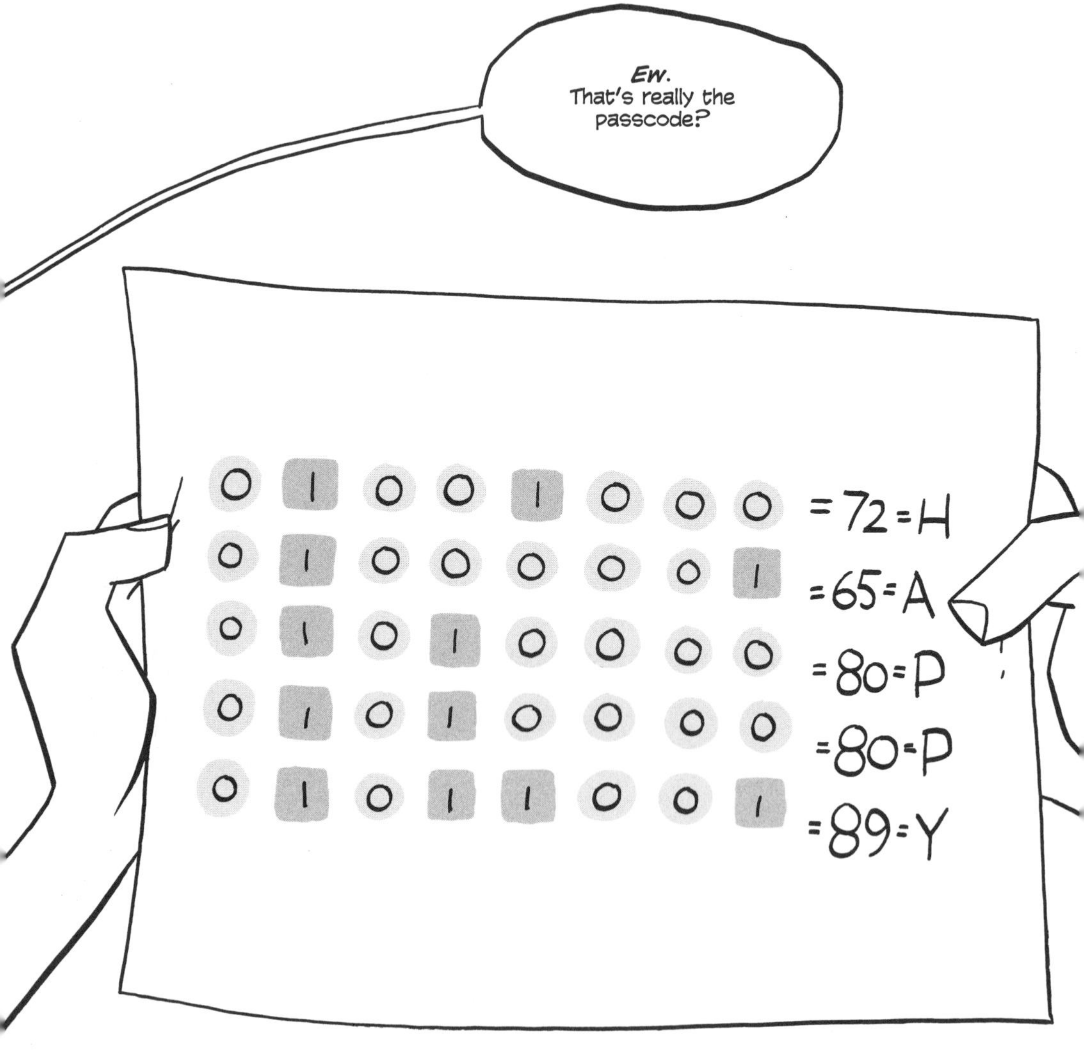
Ew. That's really the passcode?
0 1 0 0 1 0 0 0 =72=H
0 1 0 0 0 0 0 1 =65=A
0 1 0 1 0 0 0 0 =80=P
0 1 0 1 0 0 0 0 =80=P
0 1 0 1 1 0 0 1 =89=Y

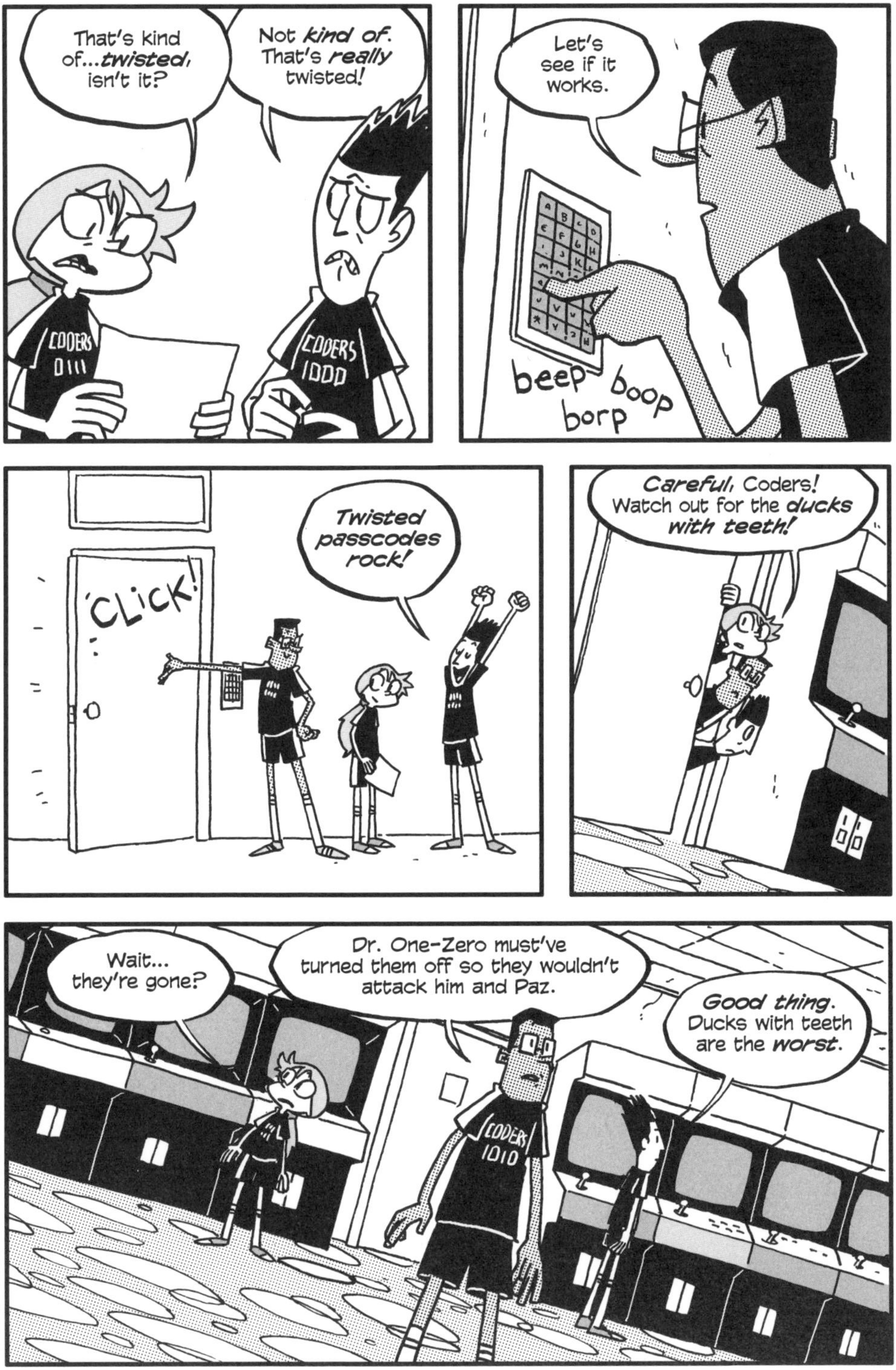
That's kind of...*twisted*, isn't it?
Not *kind of*. That's *really* twisted!
CODERS 0111
CODERS 1000
Let's see if it works.
beep borp boop
CLICK!
Twisted passcodes rock!
Careful, Coders! Watch out for the *ducks with teeth!*
Wait... they're gone?
Dr. One-Zero must've turned them off so they wouldn't attack him and Paz.
Good thing. Ducks with teeth are the *worst*.
CODERS 1010

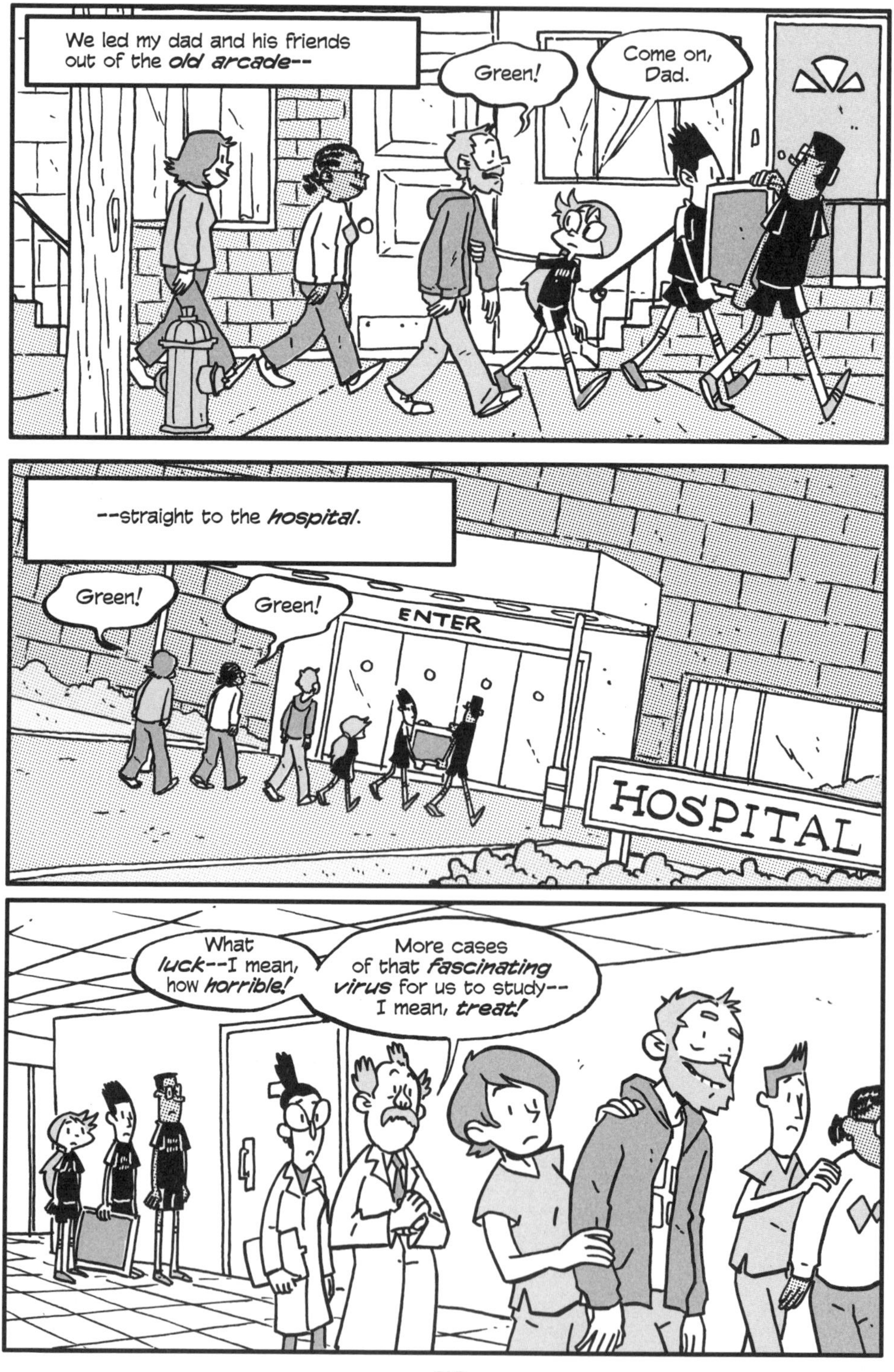
We led my dad and his friends out of the *old arcade*--
Green!
Come on, Dad.
--straight to the *hospital*.
Green!
Green!
ENTER
HOSPITAL
What *luck*--I mean, how *horrible!*
More cases of that *fascinating virus* for us to study--I mean, *treat!*

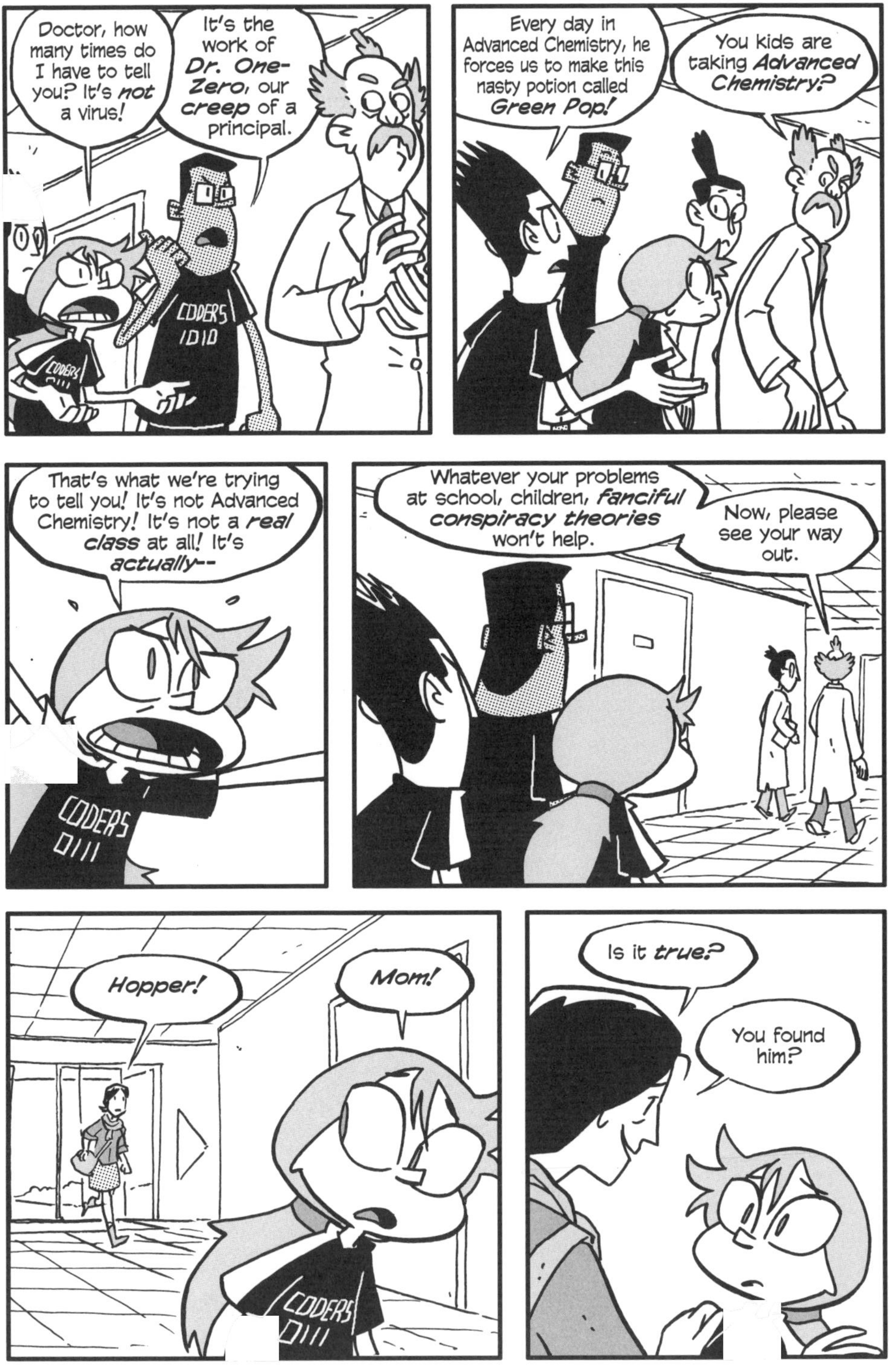
Doctor, how many times do I have to tell you? It's *not* a virus!
It's the work of *Dr. One-Zero,* our *creep* of a principal.
CODERS 1010
CODERS 0111
Every day in Advanced Chemistry, he forces us to make this nasty potion called *Green Pop!*
You kids are taking *Advanced Chemistry?*
That's what we're trying to tell you! It's not Advanced Chemistry! It's not a *real class* at all! It's *actually--*
CODERS 0111
Whatever your problems at school, children, *fanciful conspiracy theories* won't help.
Now, please see your way out.
Hopper!
Mom!
CODERS 0111
Is it *true?*
You found him?

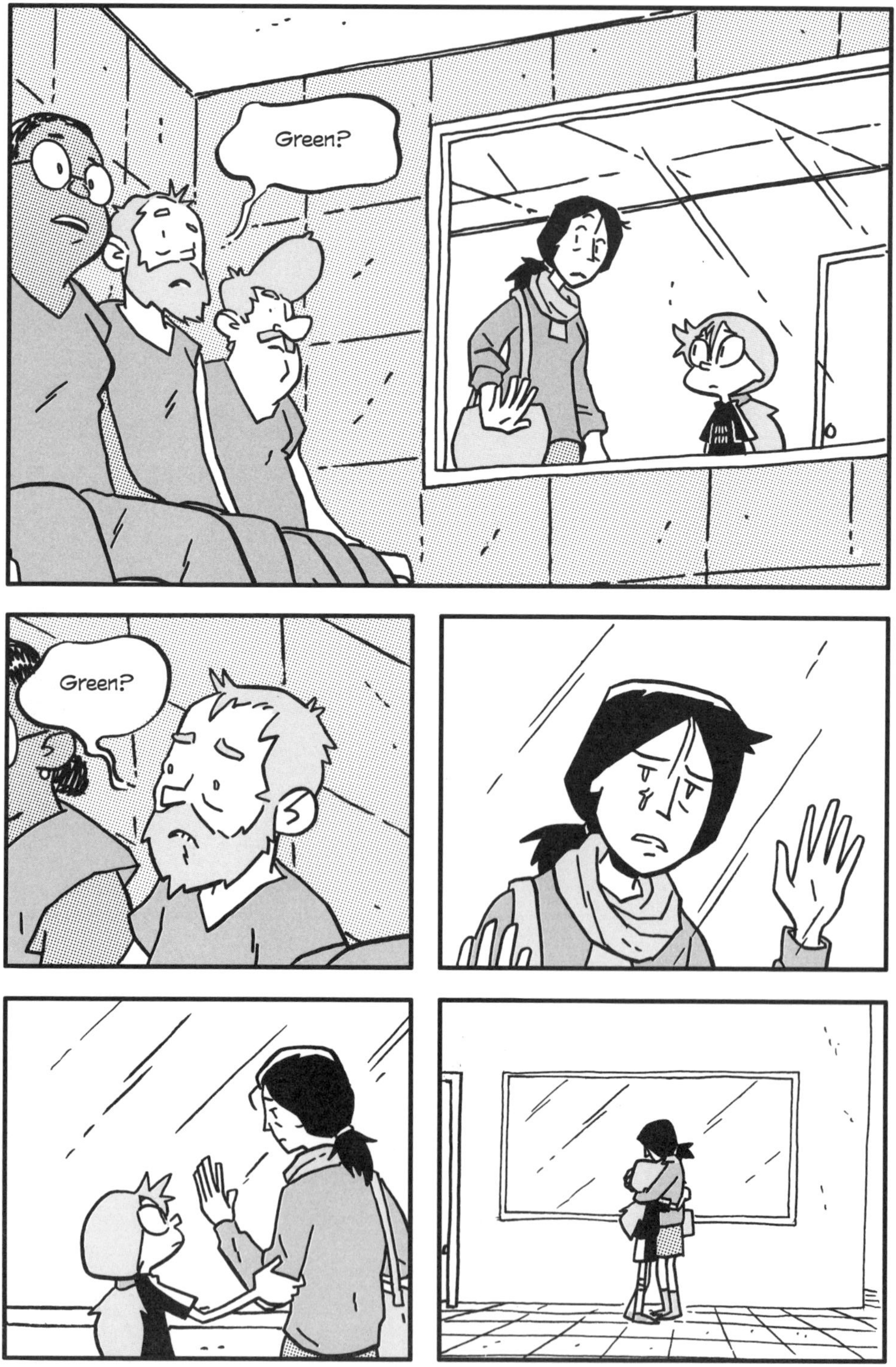
Green?
Green?

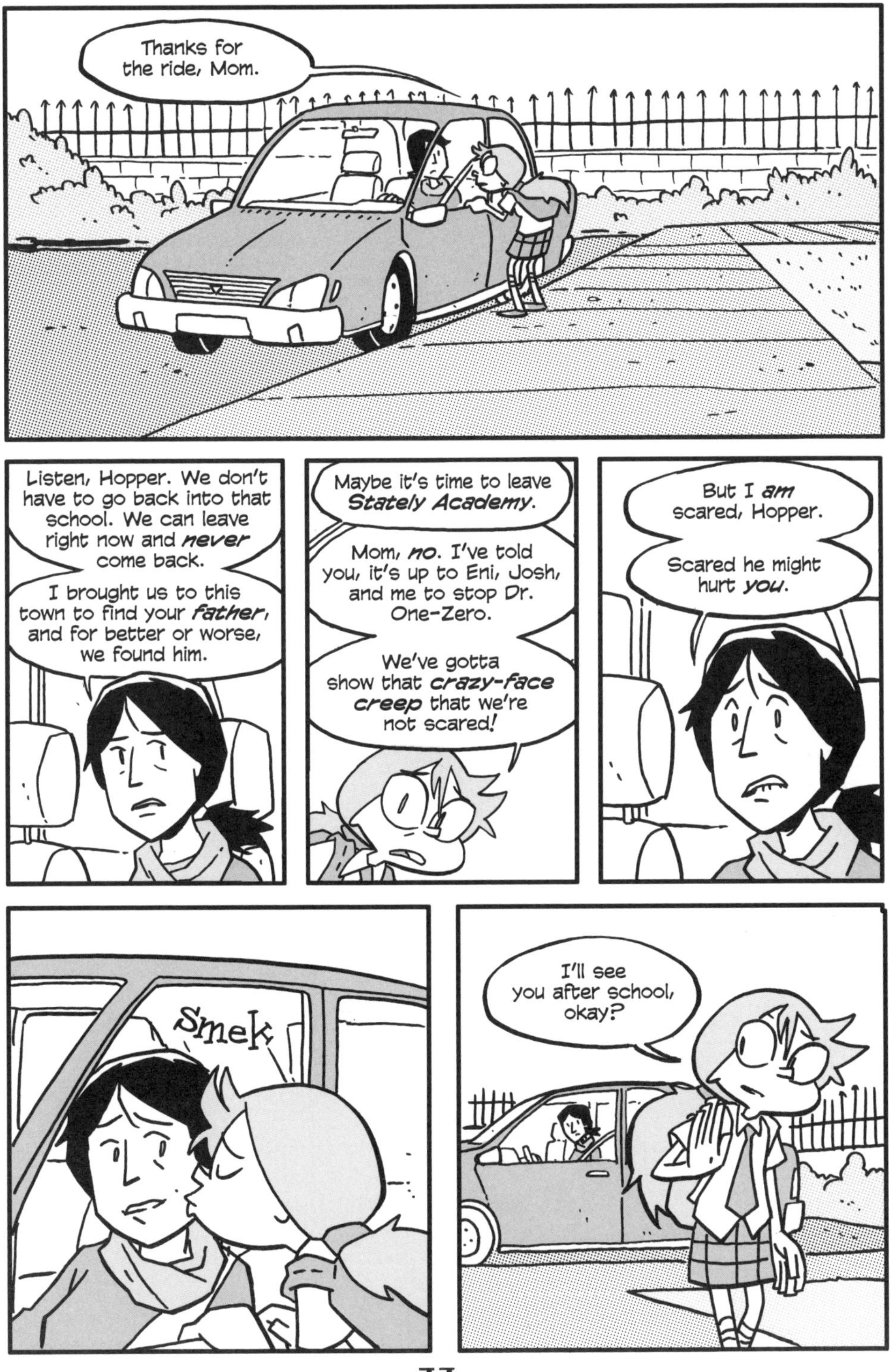

Thanks for the ride, Mom.
Listen, Hopper. We don't have to go back into that school. We can leave right now and *never* come back.
I brought us to this town to find your *father*, and for better or worse, we found him.
Maybe it's time to leave *Stately Academy*.
Mom, *no*. I've told you, it's up to Eni, Josh, and me to stop Dr. One-Zero.
We've gotta show that *crazy-face creep* that we're not scared!
But I *am* scared, Hopper.
Scared he might hurt *you*.
Smek
I'll see you after school, okay?

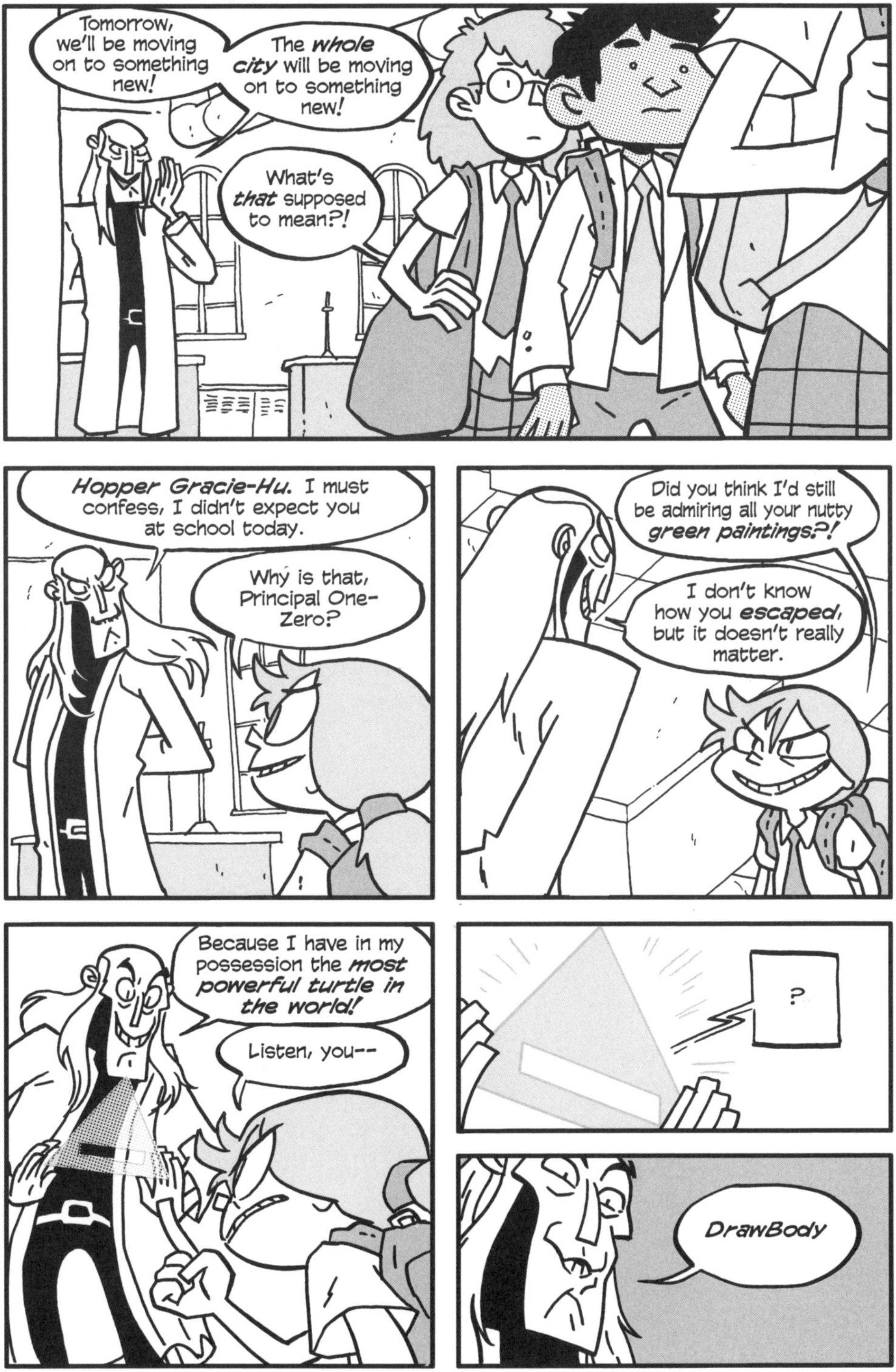
Tomorrow, we'll be moving on to something new!
The *whole city* will be moving on to something new!
What's *that* supposed to mean?!
Hopper Gracie-Hu. I must confess, I didn't expect you at school today.
Why is that, Principal One-Zero?
Did you think I'd still be admiring all your nutty *green paintings?!*
I don't know how you *escaped,* but it doesn't really matter.
Because I have in my possession the *most powerful turtle in the world!*
Listen, you--
?
DrawBody

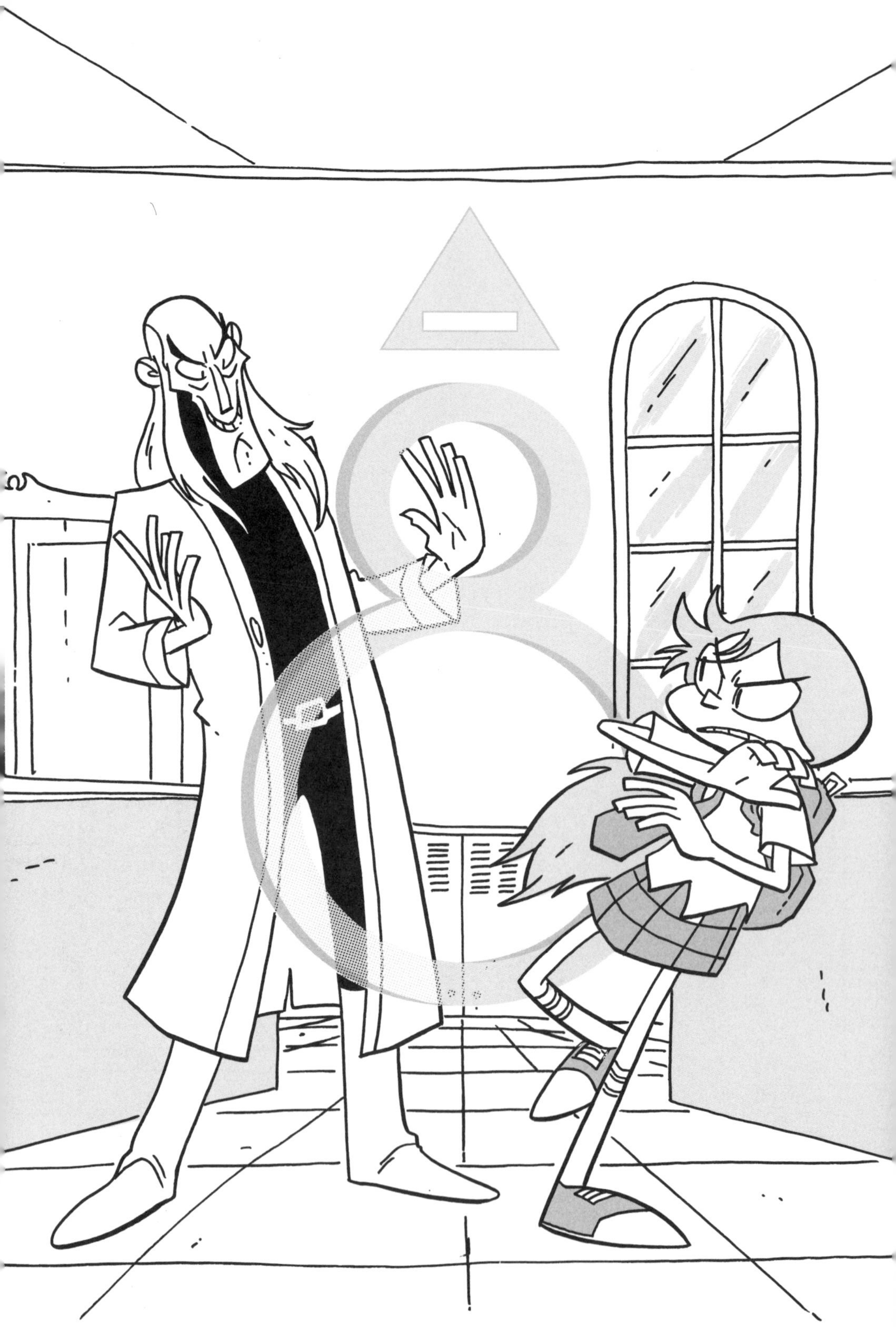

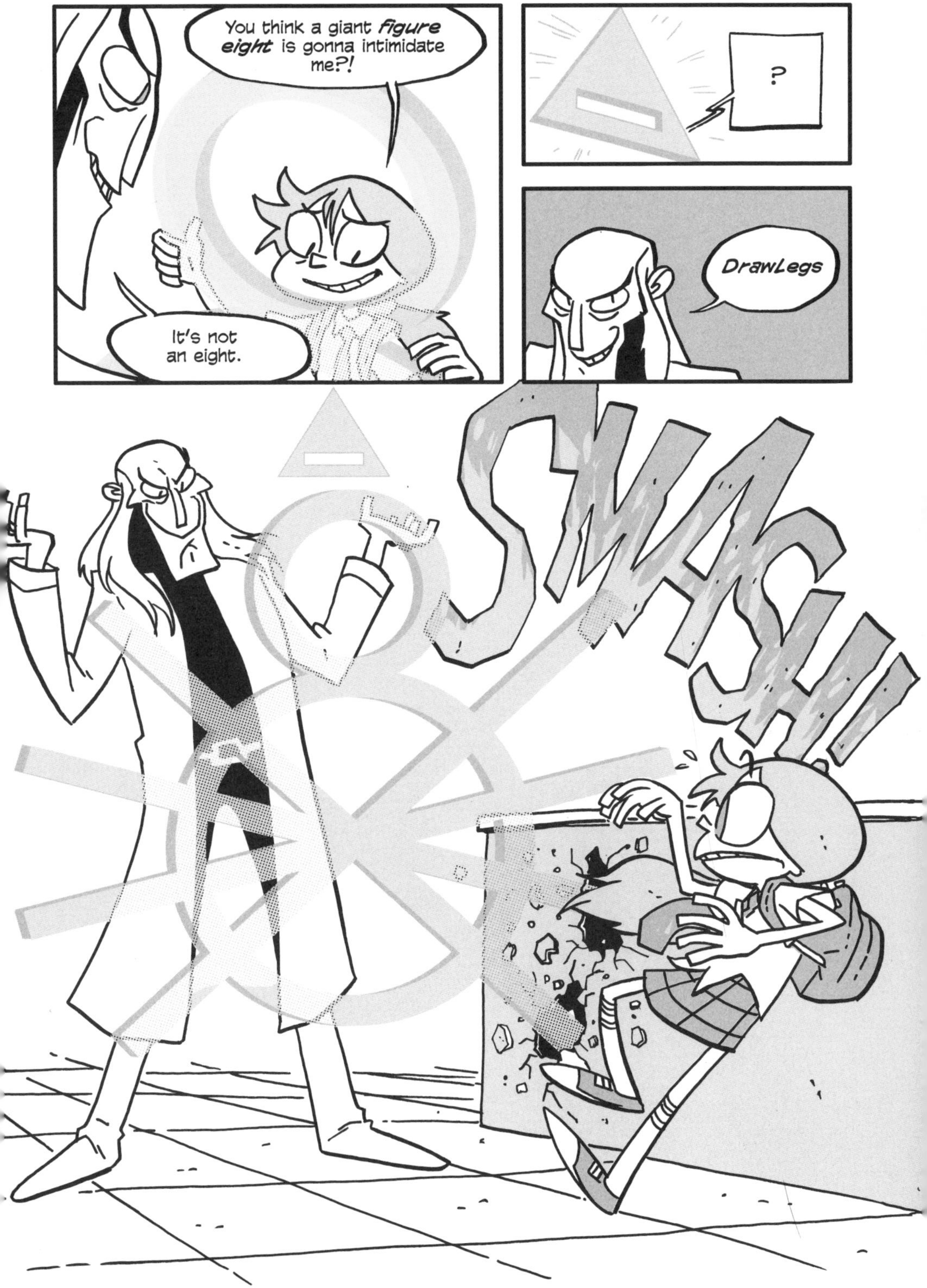

You think a giant *figure eight* is gonna intimidate me?!
It's not an eight.
?
DrawLegs
SMASH!!

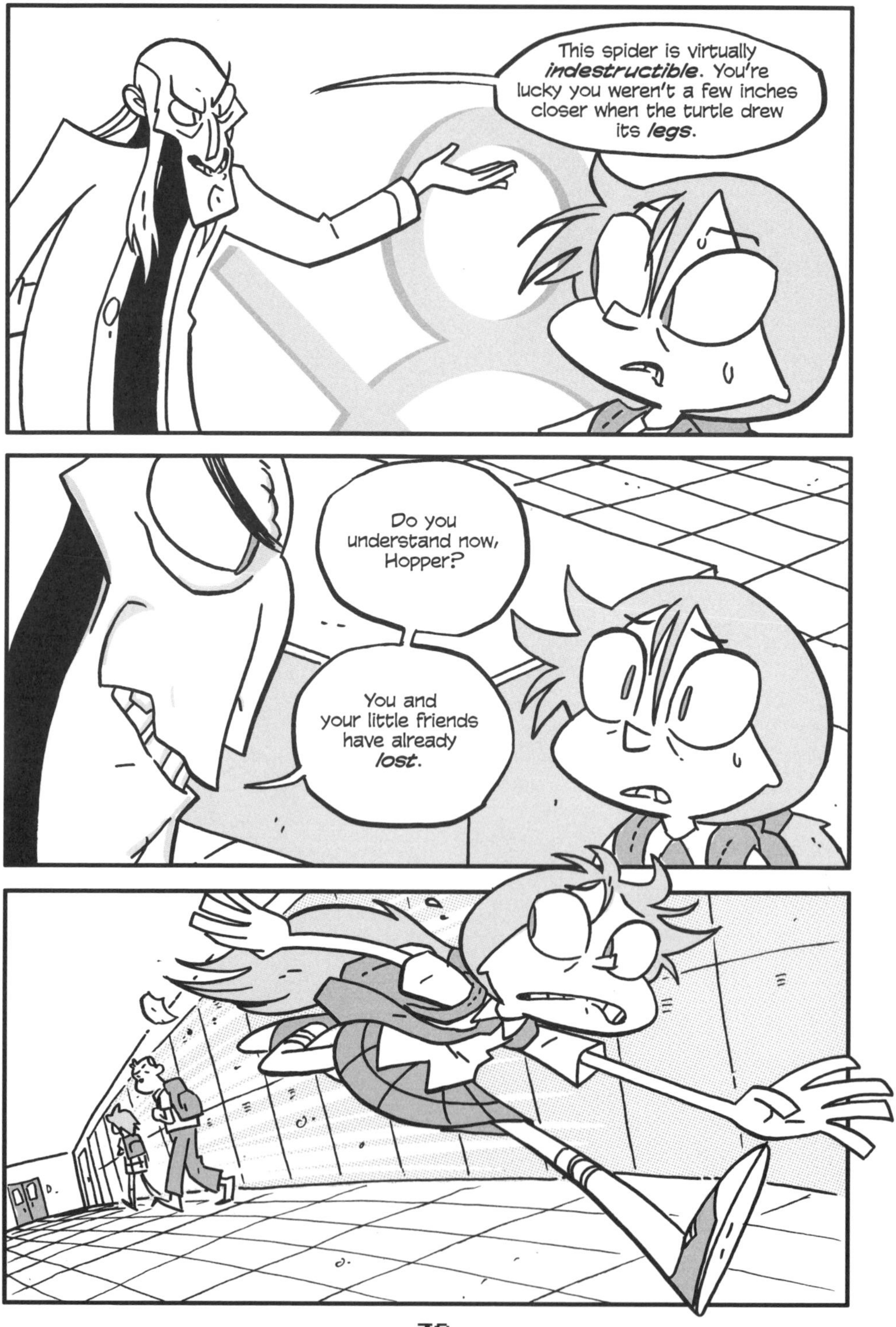
This spider is virtually *indestructible*. You're lucky you weren't a few inches closer when the turtle drew its *legs*.
Do you understand now, Hopper?
You and your little friends have already *lost*.

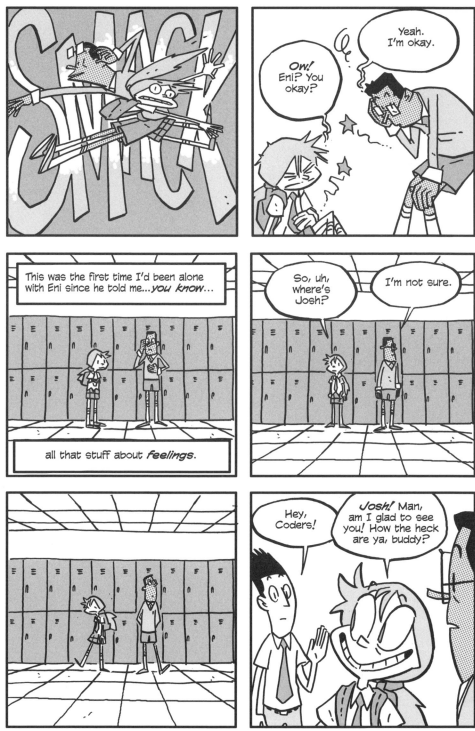

41

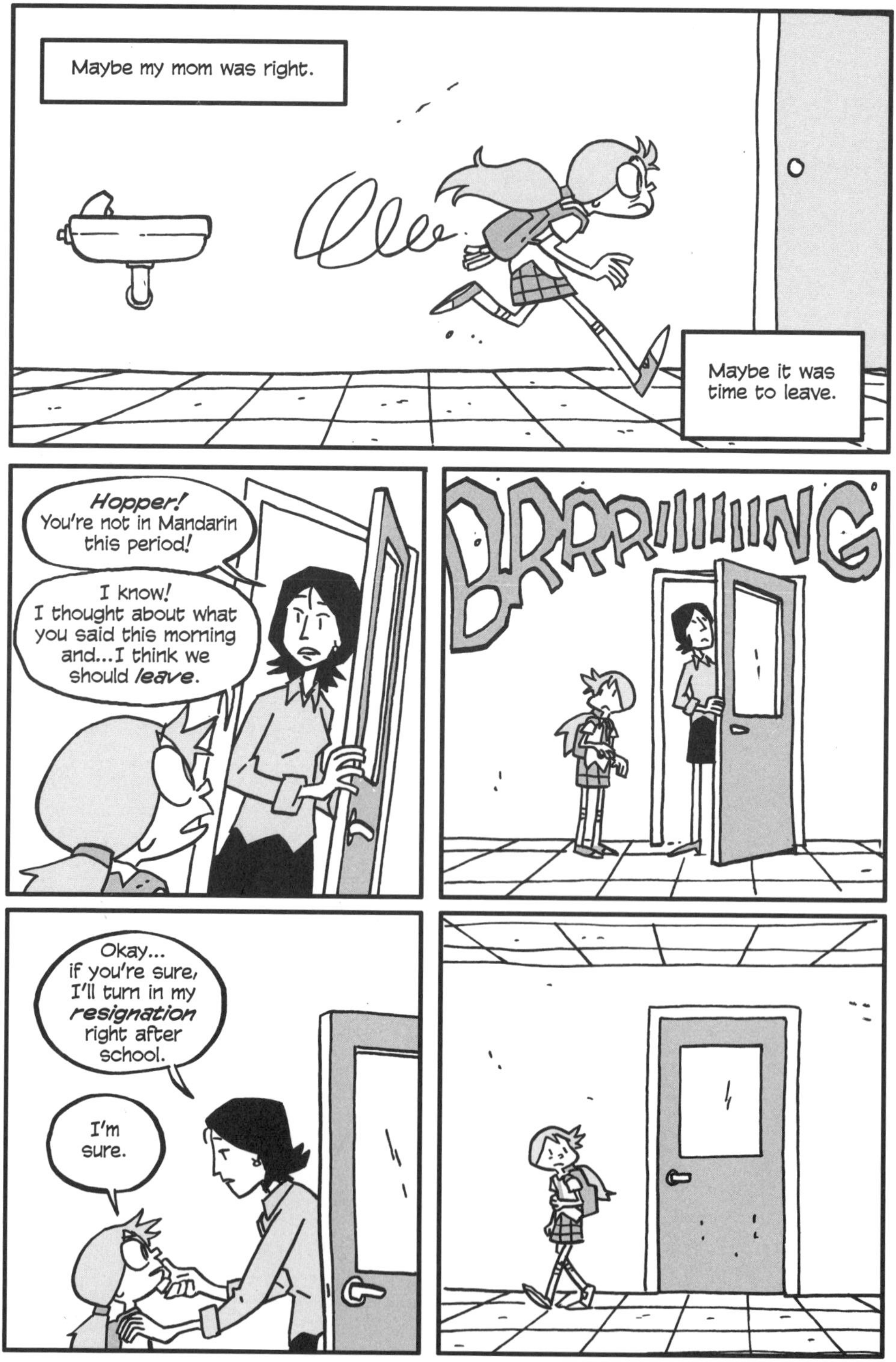
Maybe my mom was right.
Maybe it was time to leave.
Hopper! You're not in Mandarin this period!
I know! I thought about what you said this morning and...I think we should leave.
BRRRIIIIIING
Okay... if you're sure, I'll turn in my resignation right after school.
I'm sure.

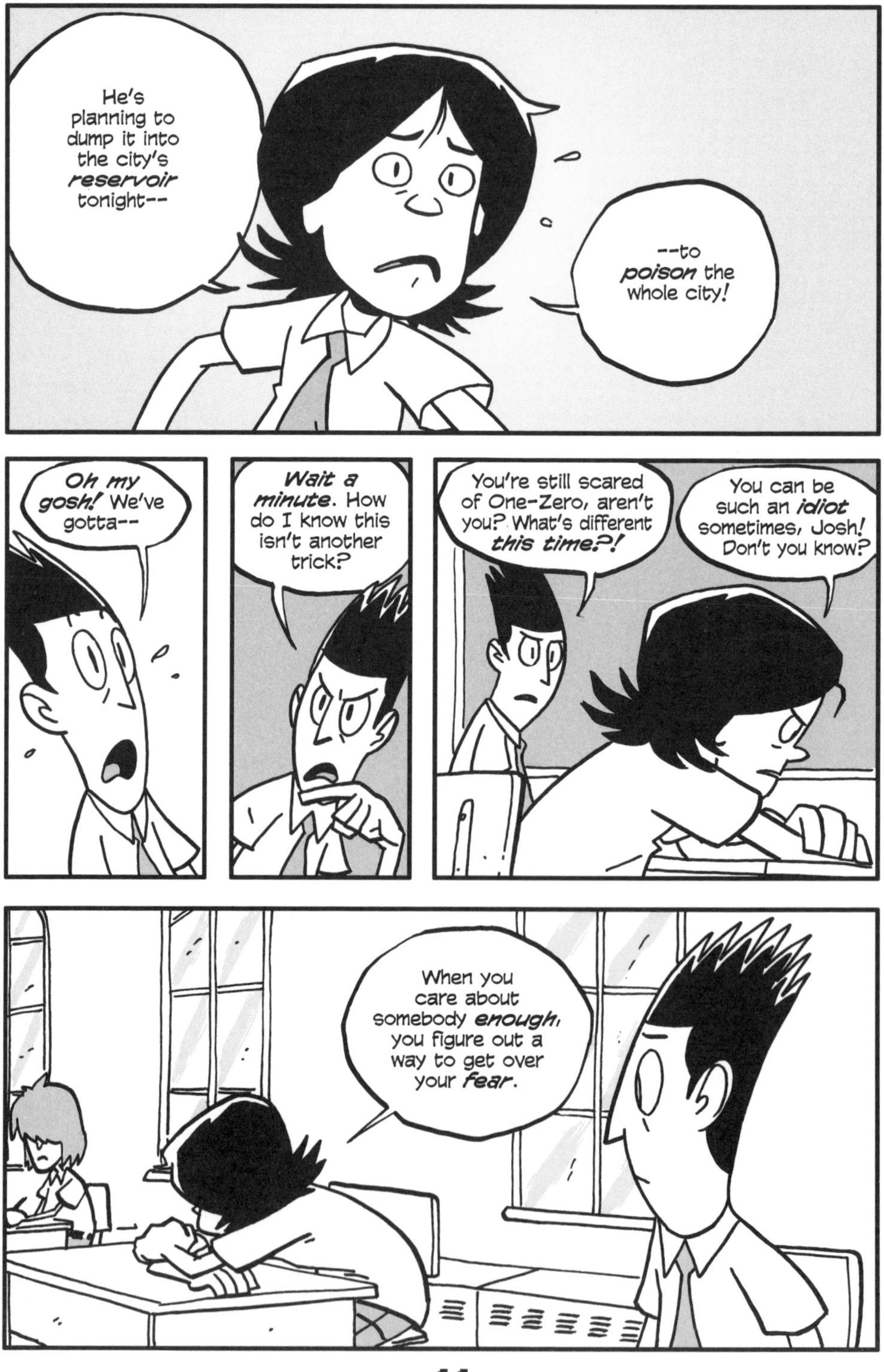
He's planning to dump it into the city's *reservoir* tonight--
--to *poison* the whole city!
Oh my gosh! We've gotta--
Wait a minute. How do I know this isn't another trick?
You're still scared of One-Zero, aren't you? What's different *this time?!*
You can be such an *idiot* sometimes, Josh! Don't you know?
When you care about somebody *enough*, you figure out a way to get over your *fear*.

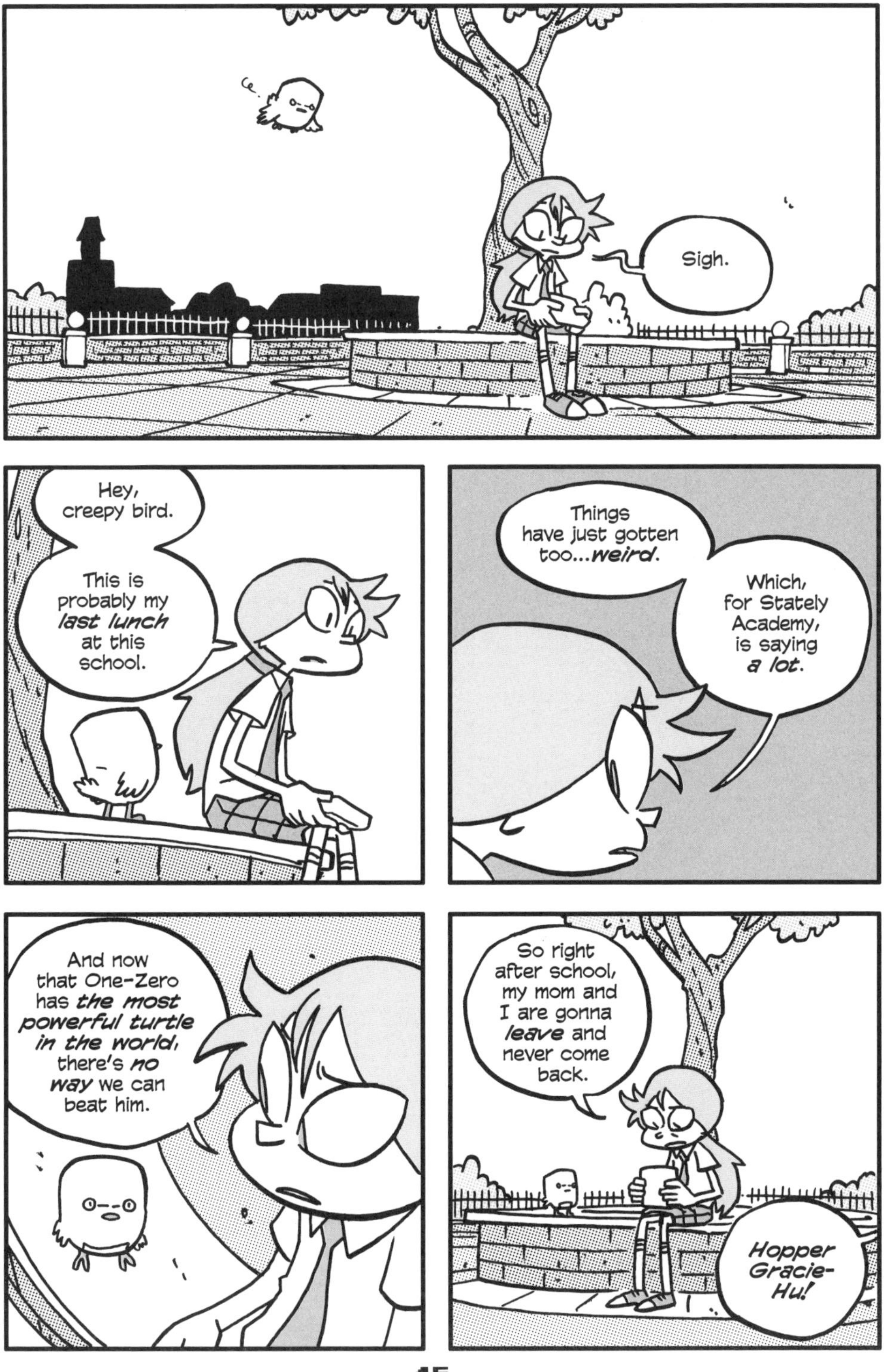
Sigh.
Hey, creepy bird.
This is probably my *last lunch* at this school.
Things have just gotten too...*weird*.
Which, for Stately Academy, is saying *a lot*.
And now that One-Zero has *the most powerful turtle in the world*, there's *no way* we can beat him.
So right after school, my mom and I are gonna *leave* and never come back.
Hopper Gracie-Hu!

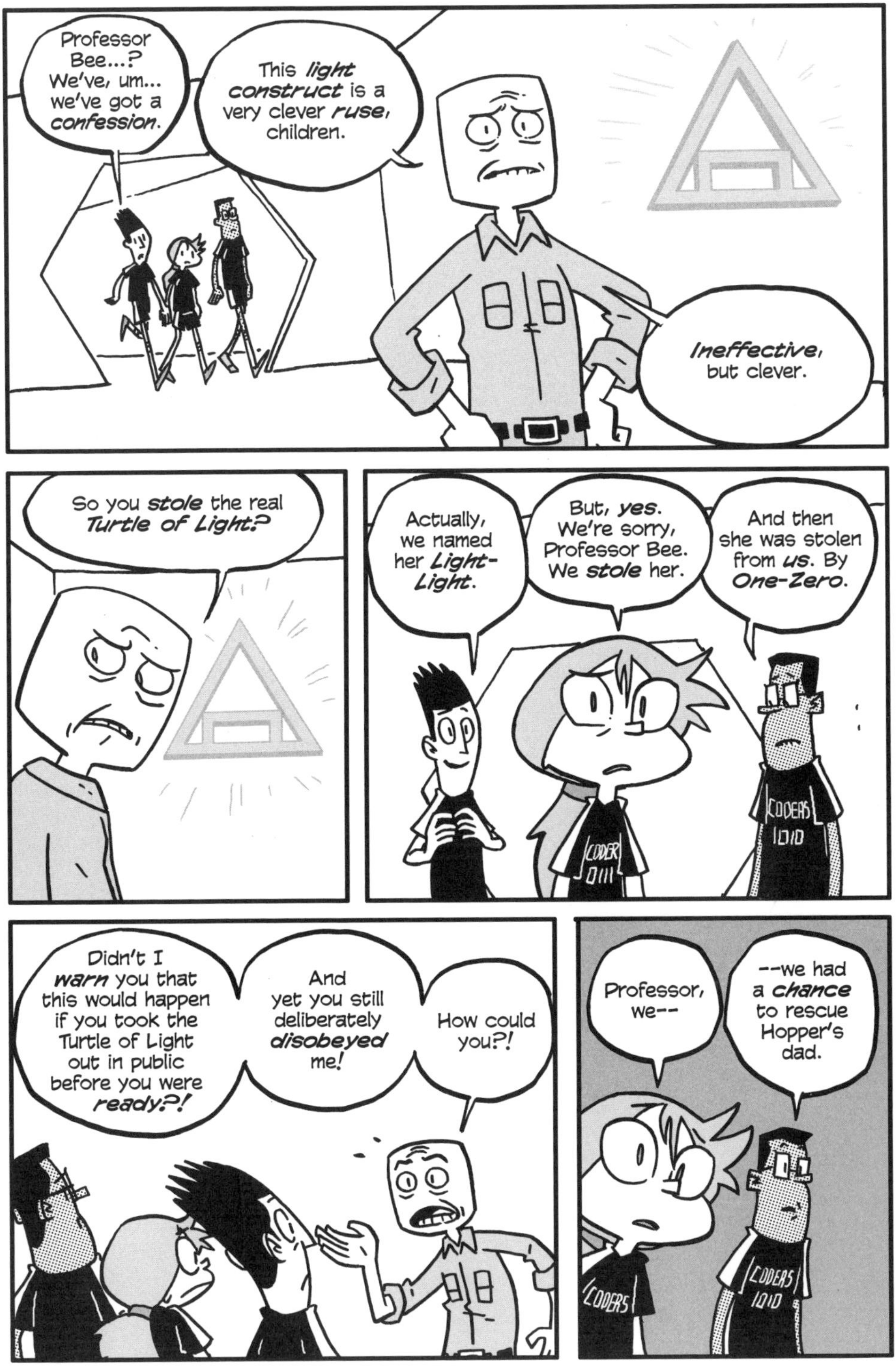
Professor Bee...? We've, um... we've got a *confession*.
This *light construct* is a very clever *ruse*, children.
Ineffective, but clever.
So you *stole* the real *Turtle of Light?*
Actually, we named her *Light-Light*.
But, *yes*. We're sorry, Professor Bee. We *stole* her.
And then she was stolen from *us*. By *One-Zero*.
CODER 0111
CODERS 1010
Didn't I *warn* you that this would happen if you took the Turtle of Light out in public before you were *ready?!*
And yet you still deliberately *disobeyed* me!
How could you?!
Professor, we--
--we had a *chance* to rescue Hopper's dad.
CODERS
CODERS 1010

48

49

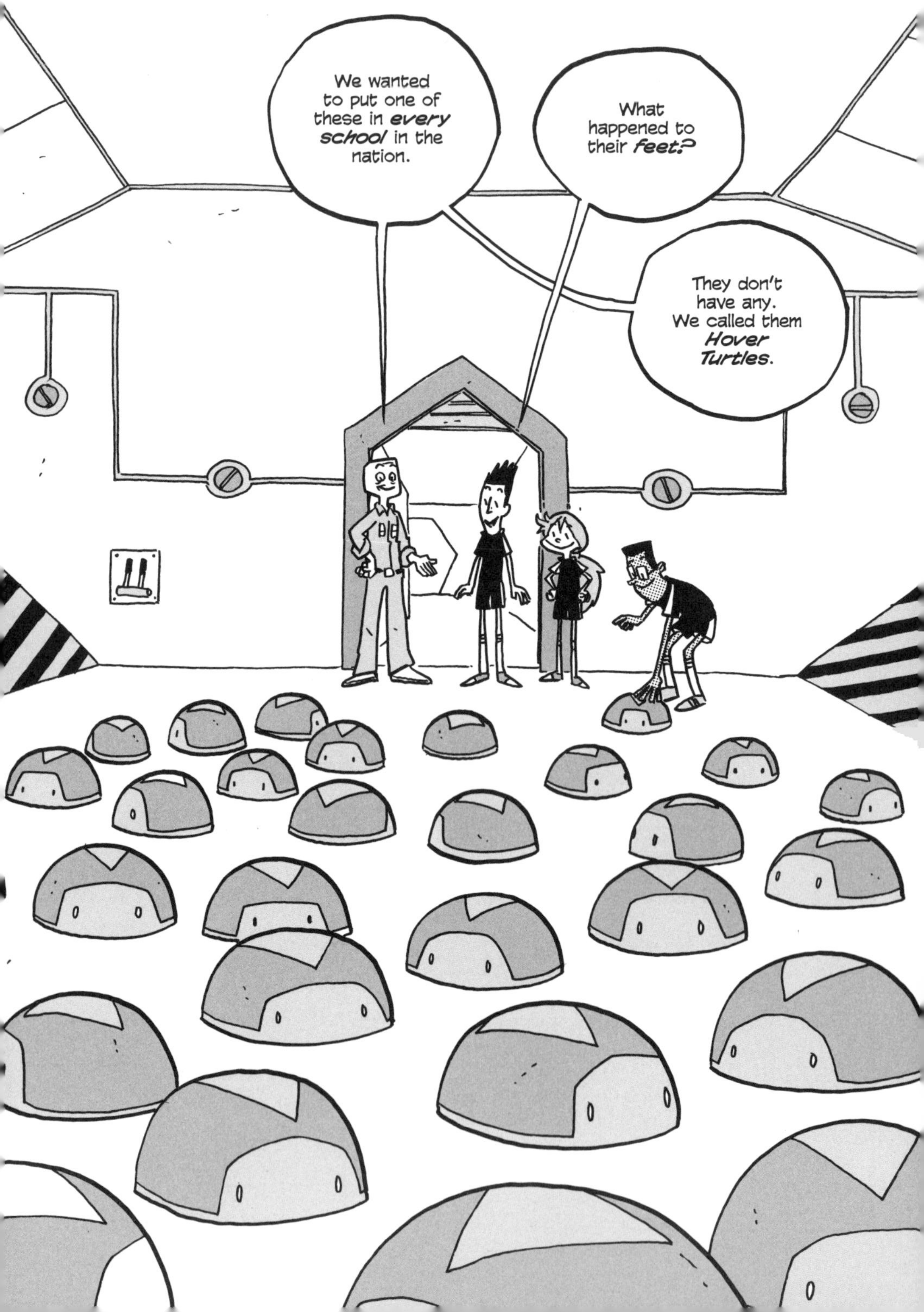
We wanted to put one of these in *every school* in the nation.
What happened to their *feet?*
They don't have any. We called them *Hover Turtles*.

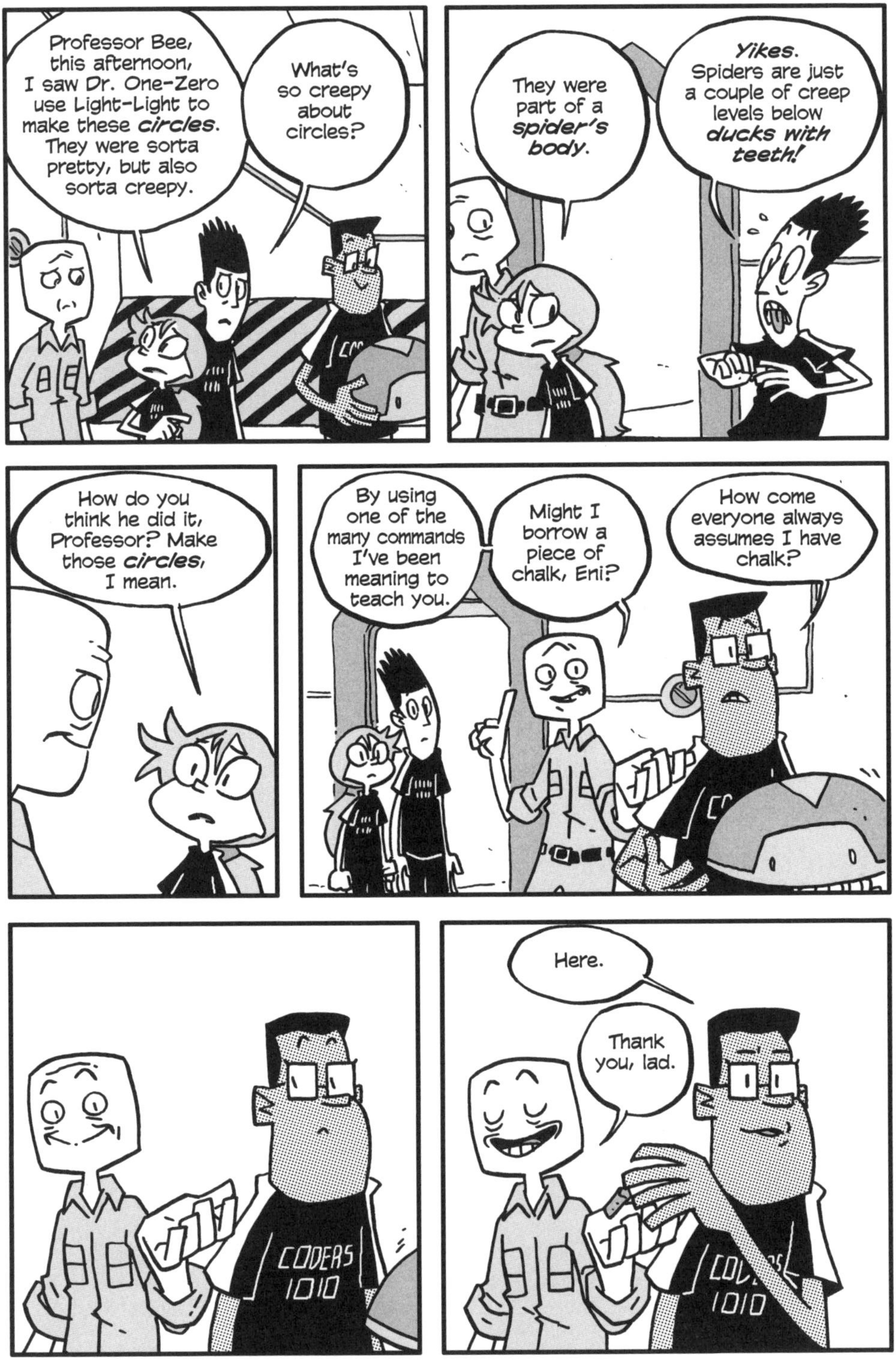
Professor Bee, this afternoon, I saw Dr. One-Zero use Light-Light to make these *circles*. They were sorta pretty, but also sorta creepy.
What's so creepy about circles?
They were part of a *spider's body*.
Yikes. Spiders are just a couple of creep levels below *ducks with teeth!*
How do you think he did it, Professor? Make those *circles*, I mean.
By using one of the many commands I've been meaning to teach you.
Might I borrow a piece of chalk, Eni?
How come everyone always assumes I have chalk?
Here.
Thank you, lad.
CODERS 1010

The *Arc* command can draw a circle or a part of a circle. It has two *parameters*.

The first tells the turtle *how much* of a circle to draw. A circle has 360 degrees, so if you were to write 360 here, it would draw an *entire circle*.

But you wrote 180. Does that mean it will just draw *half* a circle?

Precisely, Eni!

The second number tells the turtle the circle's *radius*.

"The radius is the distance from the circle's center to its outside edge.

RADIUS

"The larger the *radius*, the larger the circle!"

And when it's finished, the turtle goes back to the circle's center!

Us three in an underground classroom... Professor Bee explaining some piece of code... It feels like old times!

Except if we fail, the whole city gets *poisoned*.

Well, yeah. There's that.

That and the fact that things were *so weird* between Eni and me.

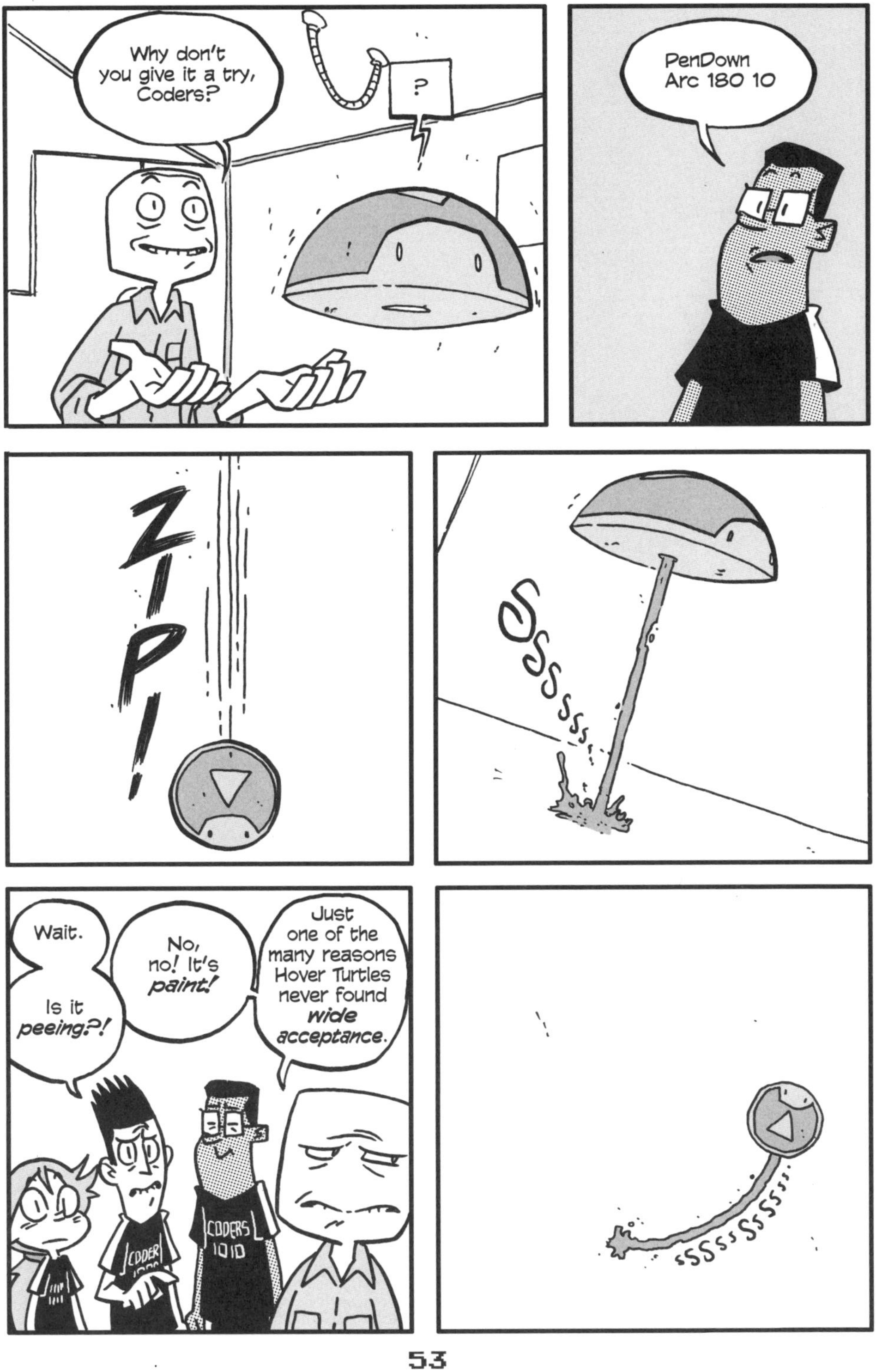
Why don't you give it a try, Coders?
?
PenDown Arc 180 10
ZIP!
Wait.
Is it *peeing?!*
No, no! It's *paint!*
Just one of the many reasons Hover Turtles never found ***wide acceptance***.
CODERS 1010

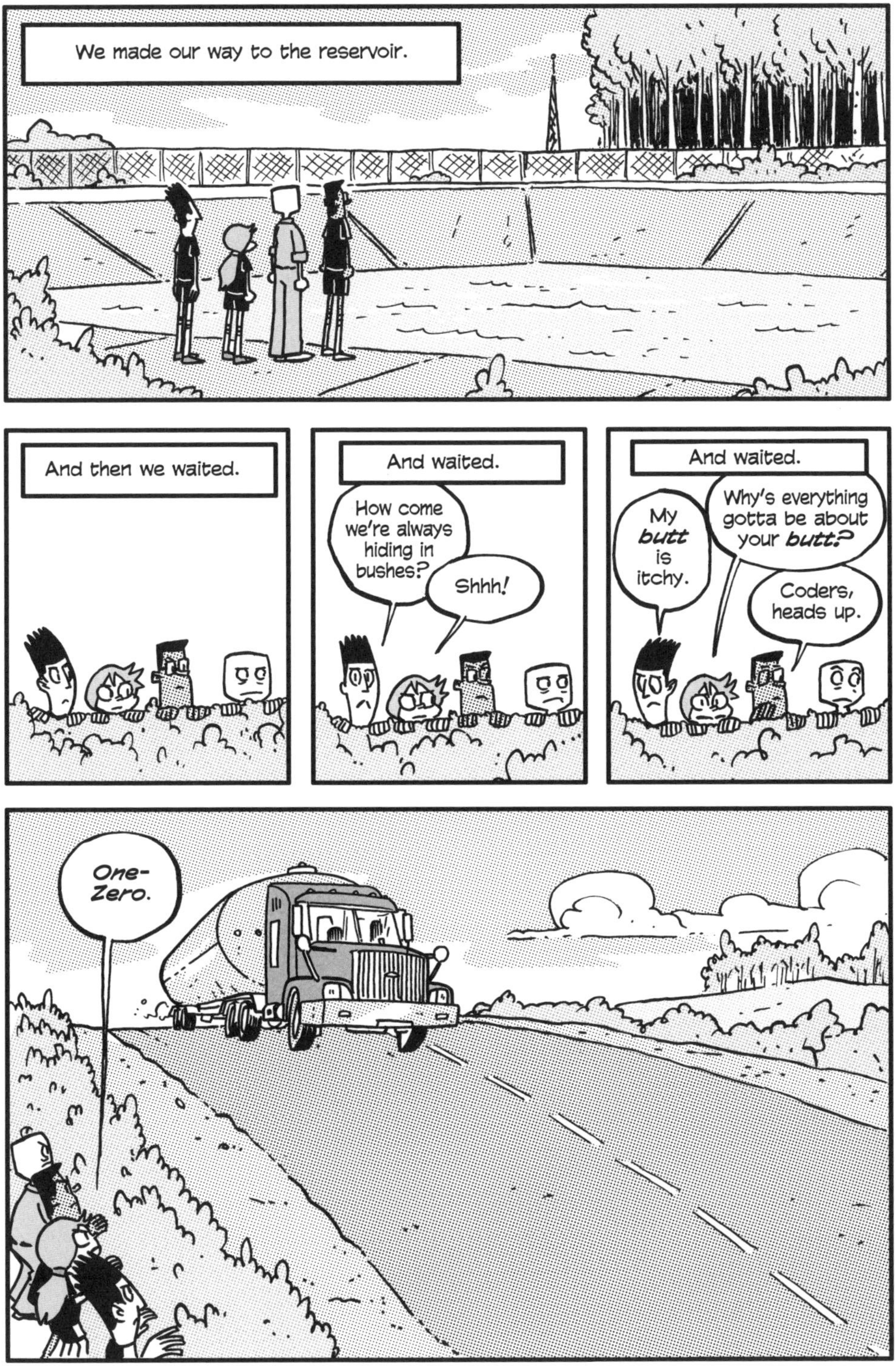
We made our way to the reservoir.
And then we waited.
And waited.
How come we're always hiding in bushes?
Shhh!
And waited.
My *butt* is itchy.
Why's everything gotta be about your *butt?*
Coders, heads up.
One-Zero.

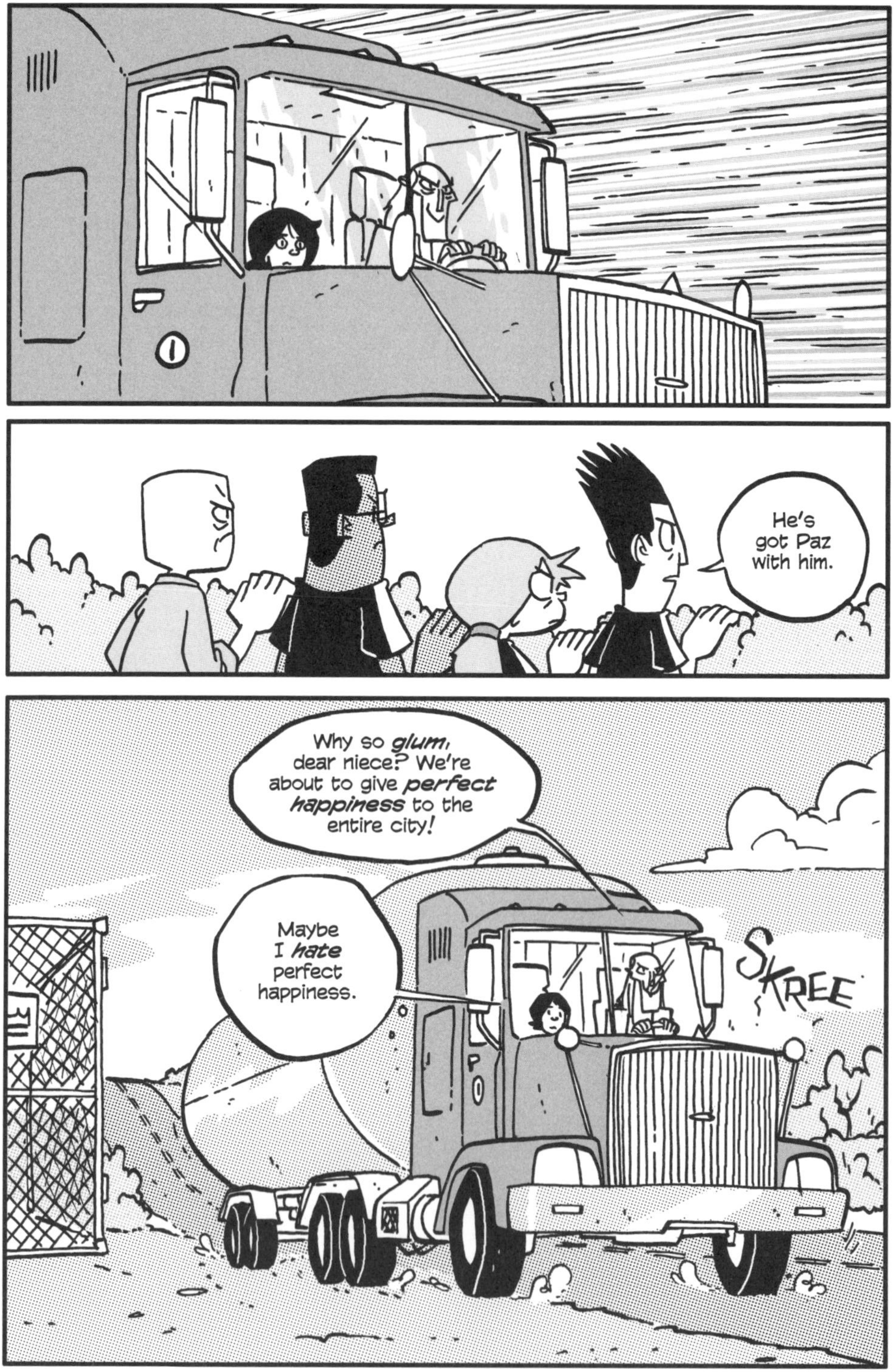
He's got Paz with him.
Why so *glum*, dear niece? We're about to give ***perfect happiness*** to the entire city!
Maybe I ***hate*** perfect happiness.
SKREE

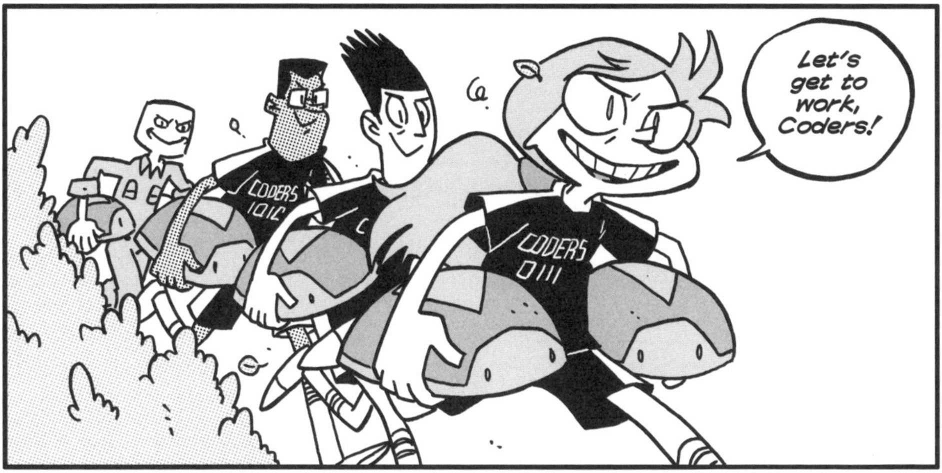
Let's get to work, Coders!
CODERS 1010
CODERS 0111

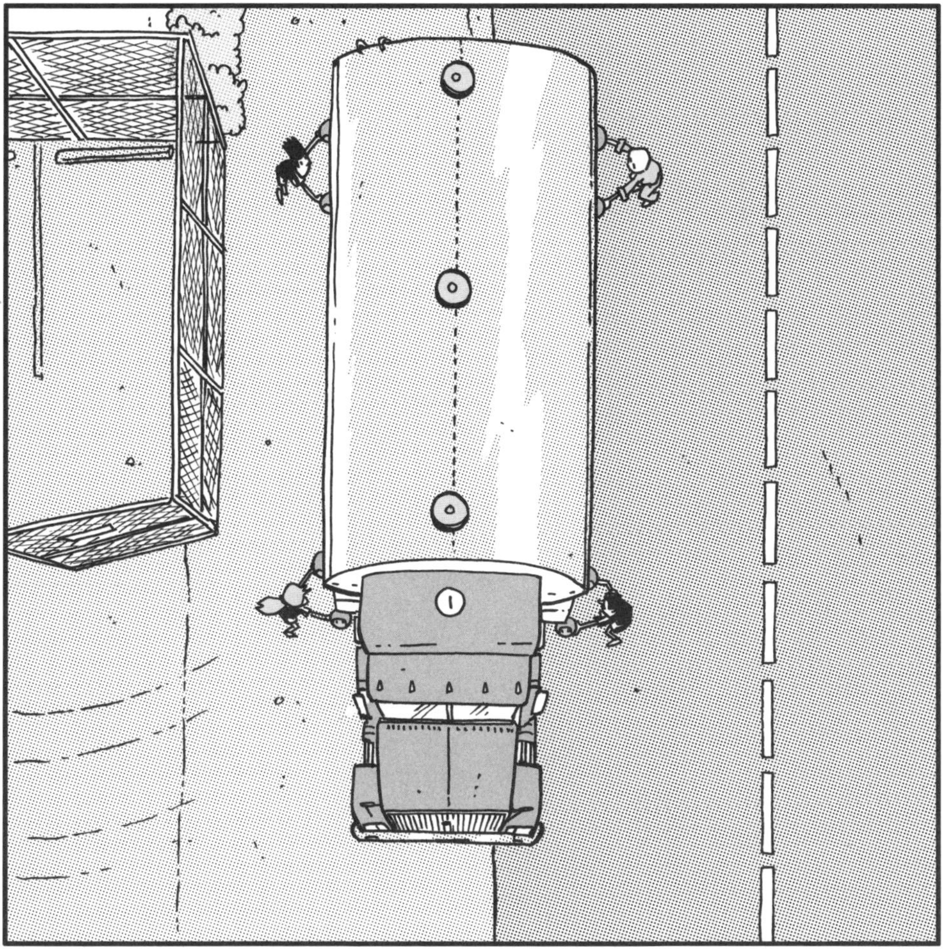

Chapter

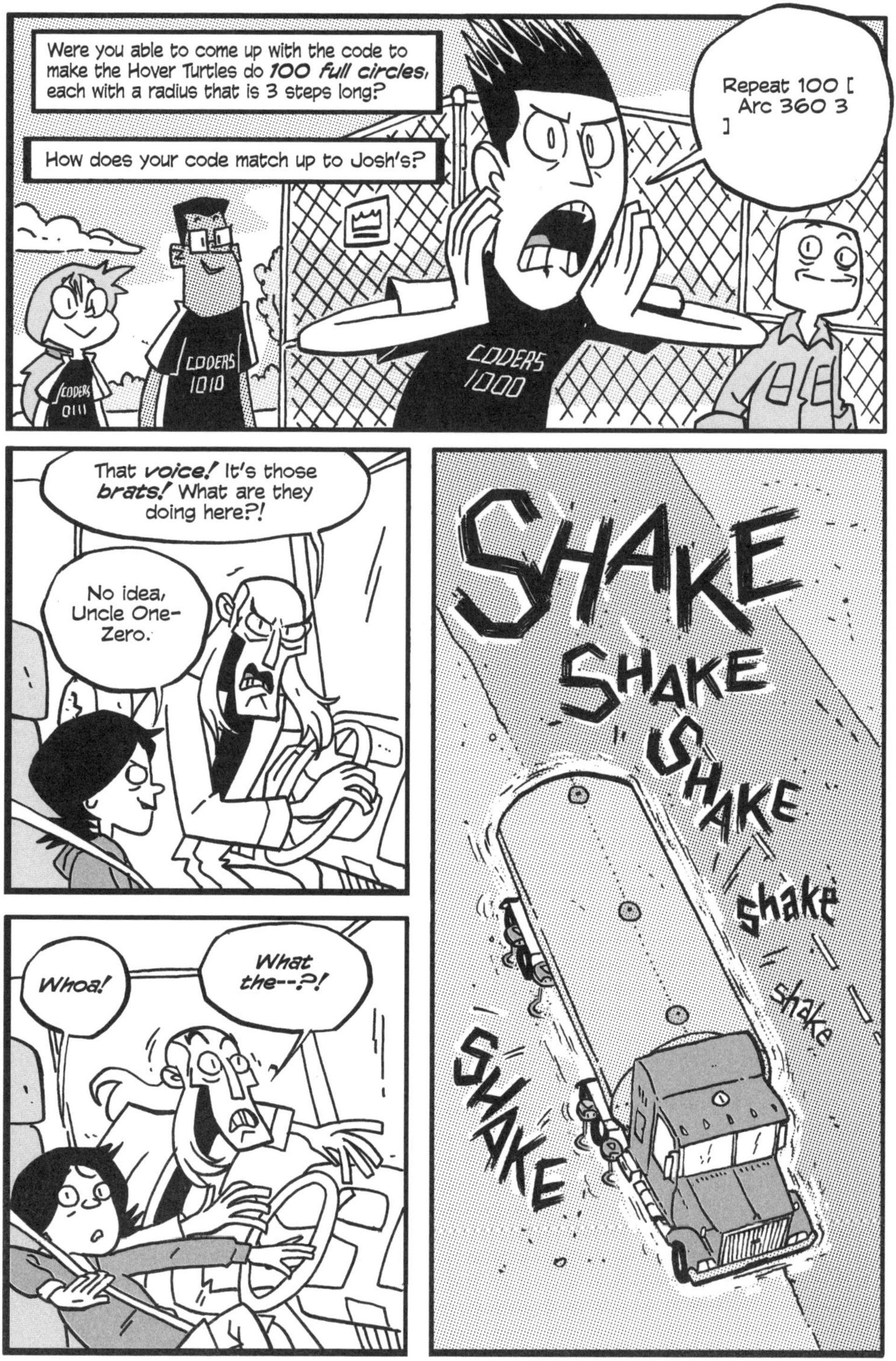
Were you able to come up with the code to make the Hover Turtles do *100 full circles*, each with a radius that is 3 steps long?
How does your code match up to Josh's?
Repeat 100 [Arc 360 3]
CODERS 0111
CODERS 1010
CODERS 1000
That *voice!* It's those *brats!* What are they doing here?!
No idea, Uncle One-Zero.
SHAKE
SHAKE
SHAKE
shake
shake
SHAKE
Whoa!
What the--?!

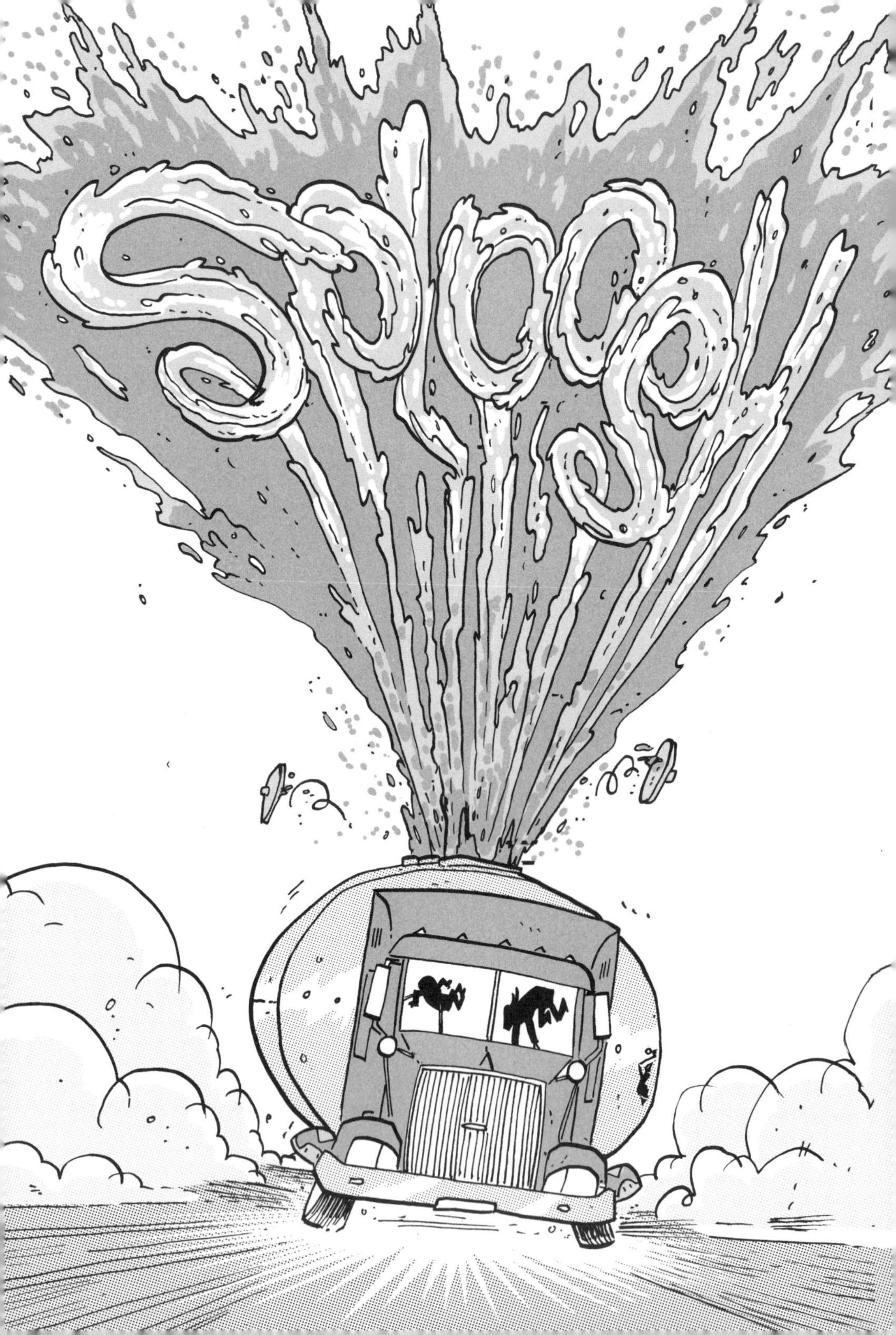

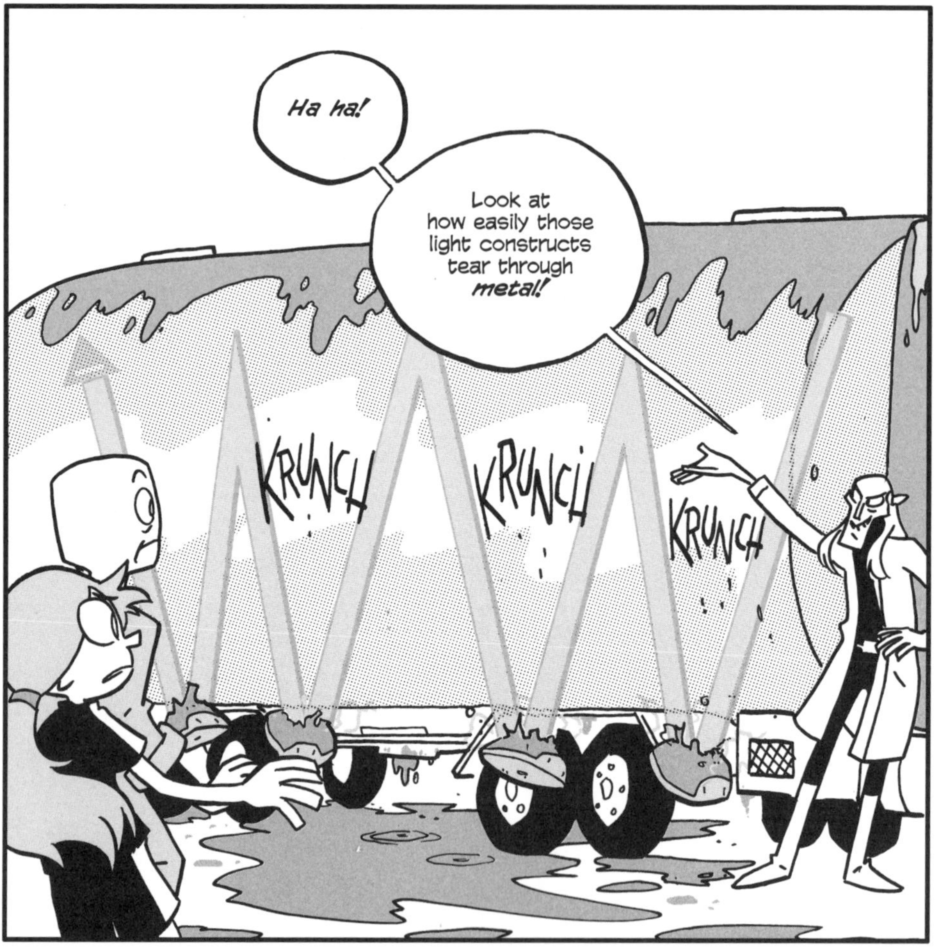
Ha ha!
Look at how easily those light constructs tear through *metal!*
KRUNCH
KRUNCH
KRUNCH

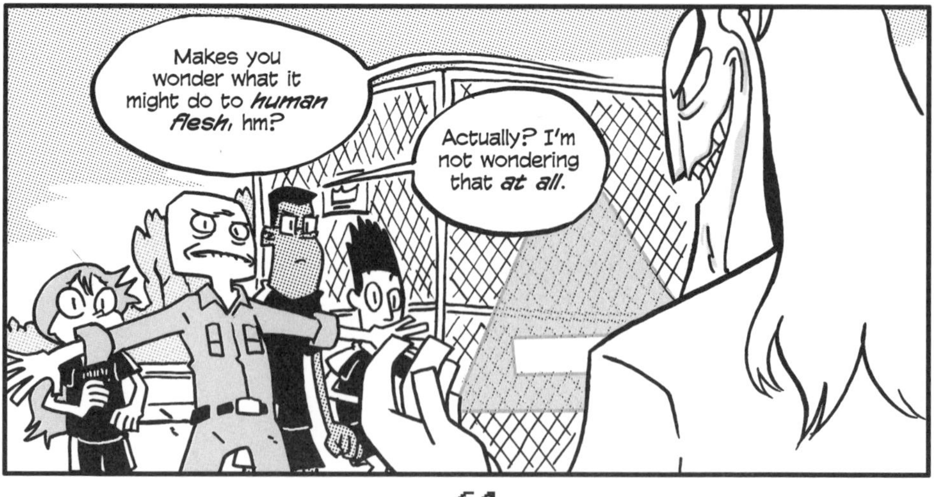
Makes you wonder what it might do to *human flesh*, hm?
Actually? I'm not wondering that *at all*.

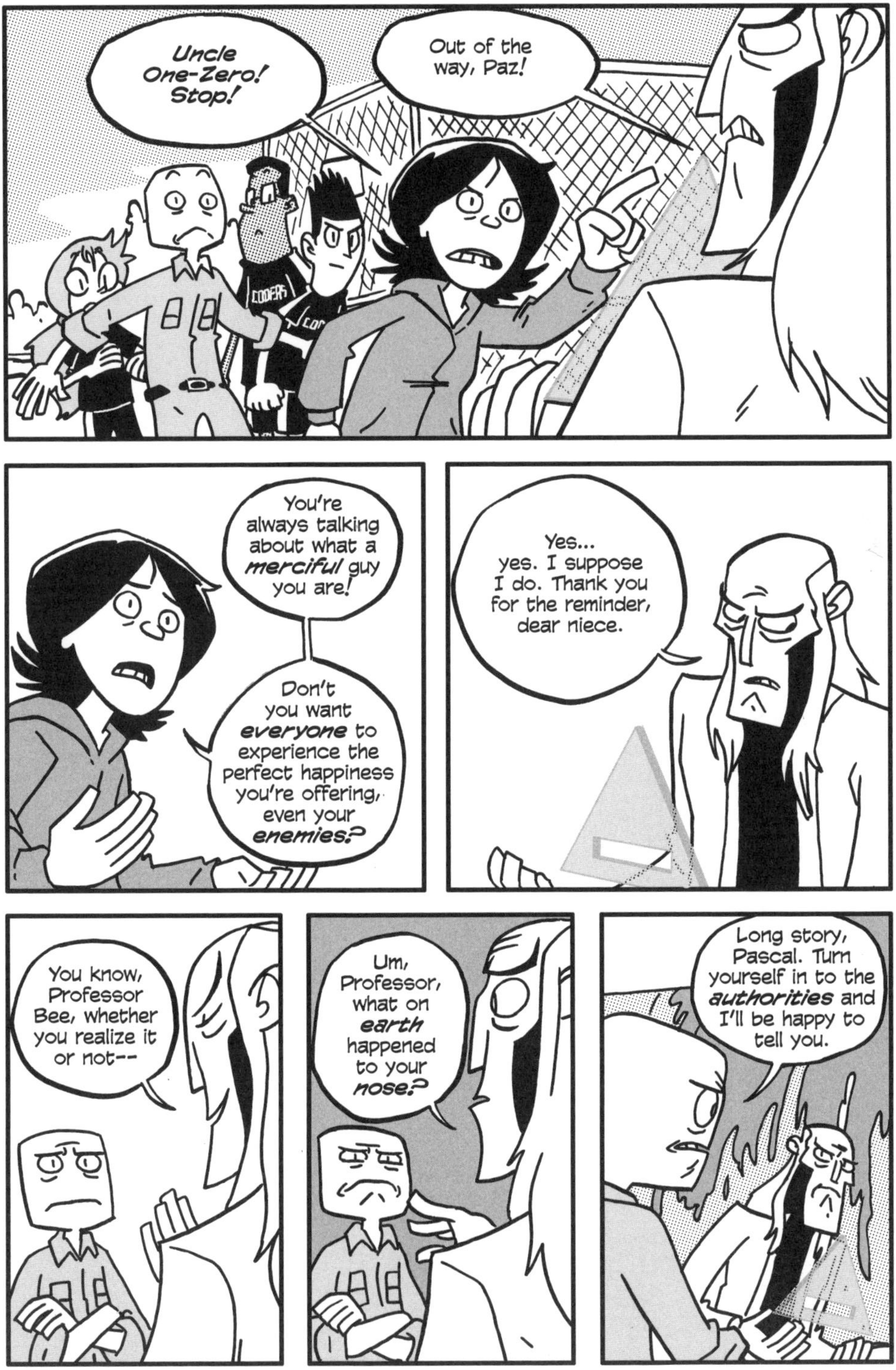
Uncle One-Zero! Stop!
Out of the way, Paz!
You're always talking about what a *merciful* guy you are!
Don't you want *everyone* to experience the perfect happiness you're offering, even your *enemies?*
Yes... yes. I suppose I do. Thank you for the reminder, dear niece.
You know, Professor Bee, whether you realize it or not--
Um, Professor, what on *earth* happened to your *nose?*
Long story, Pascal. Turn yourself in to the *authorities* and I'll be happy to tell you.

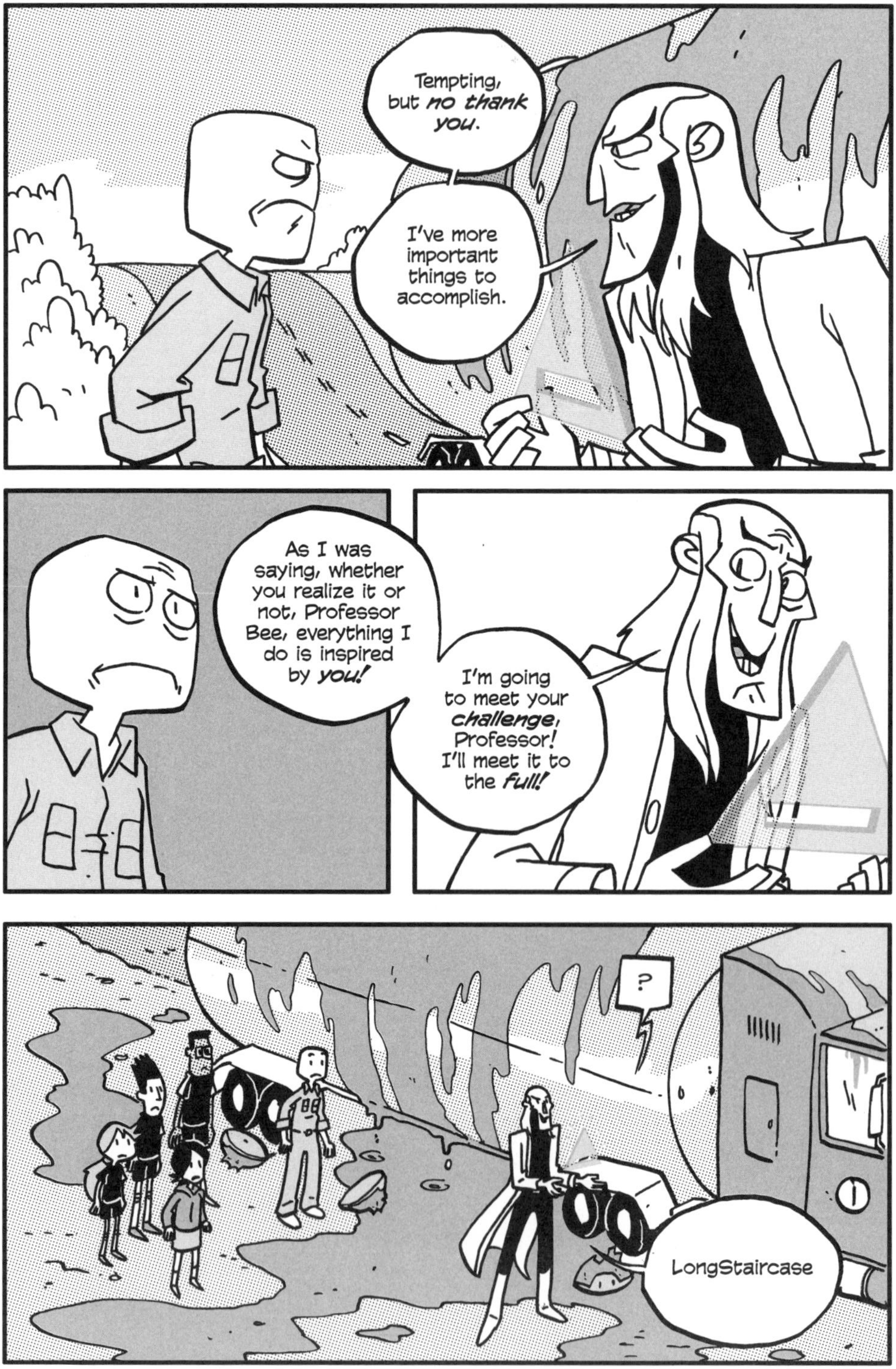
Tempting, but *no thank you*.
I've more important things to accomplish.
As I was saying, whether you realize it or not, Professor Bee, everything I do is inspired by *you!*
I'm going to meet your *challenge*, Professor! I'll meet it to the *full!*
?
LongStaircase

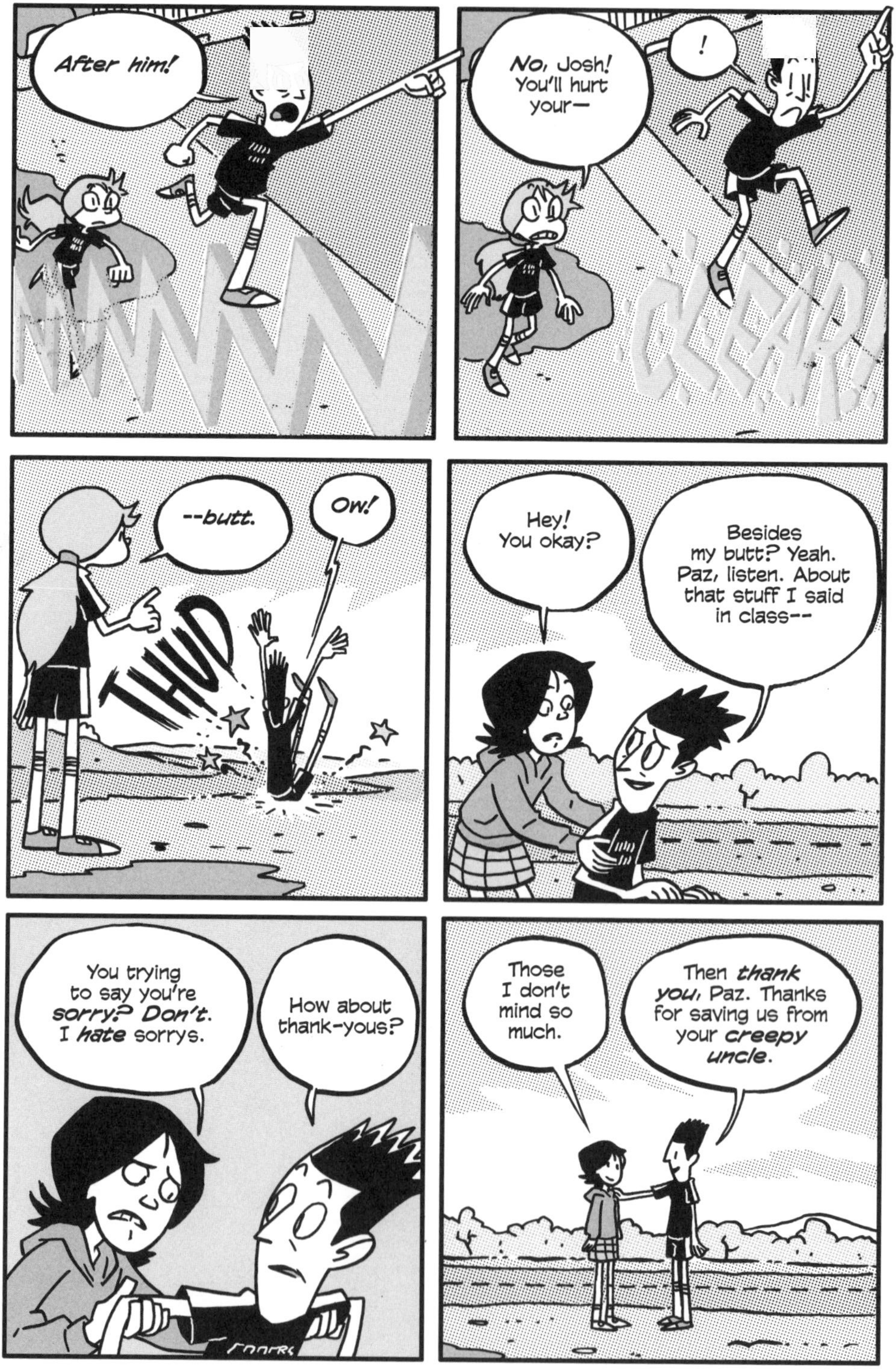
After him!
No, Josh! You'll hurt your—
!
--butt.
Ow!
THUD
Hey! You okay?
Besides my butt? Yeah. Paz, listen. About that stuff I said in class--
You trying to say you're *sorry? Don't*. I *hate* sorrys.
How about thank-yous?
Those I don't mind so much.
Then *thank you*, Paz. Thanks for saving us from your *creepy uncle*.

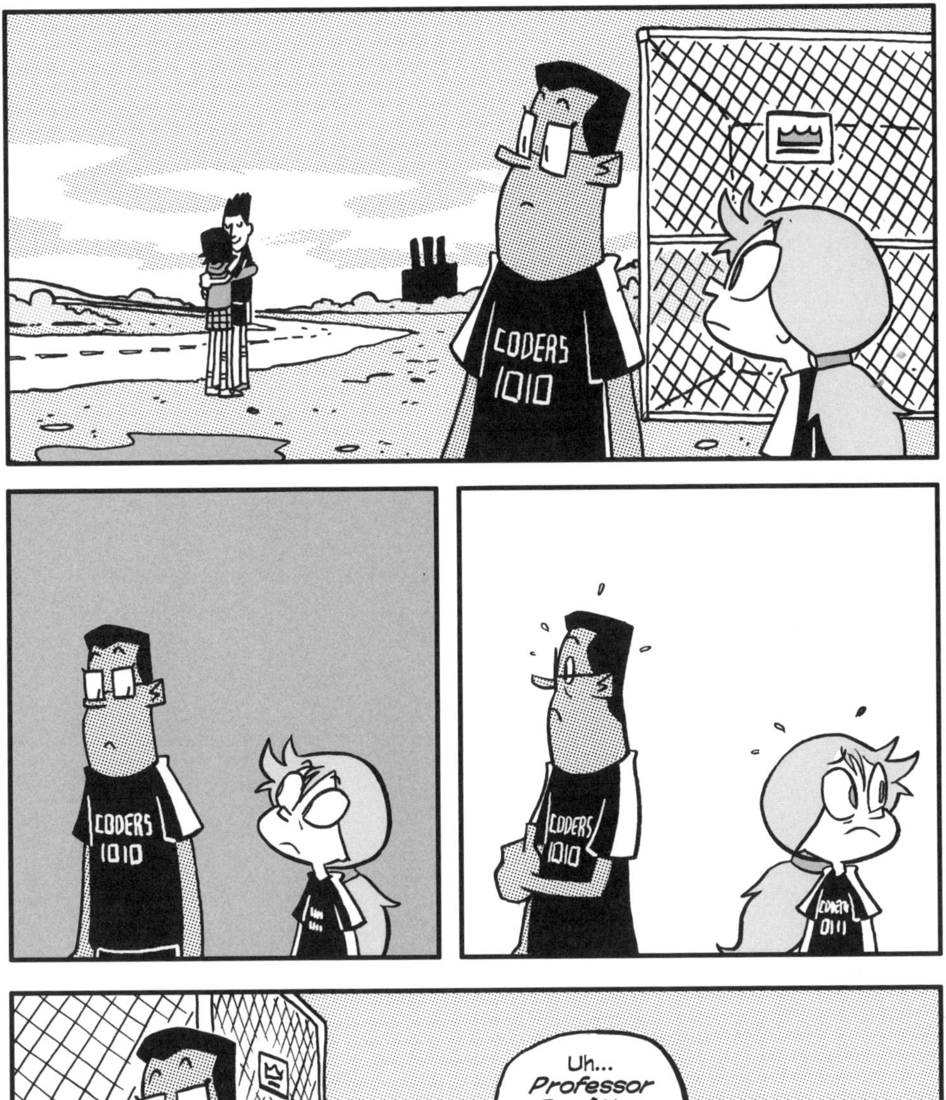
CODERS 1010
CODERS 1010
CODERS 1010
CODERS 1010
Uh... *Professor Bee!* Hey, there! Whatcha doin'?!

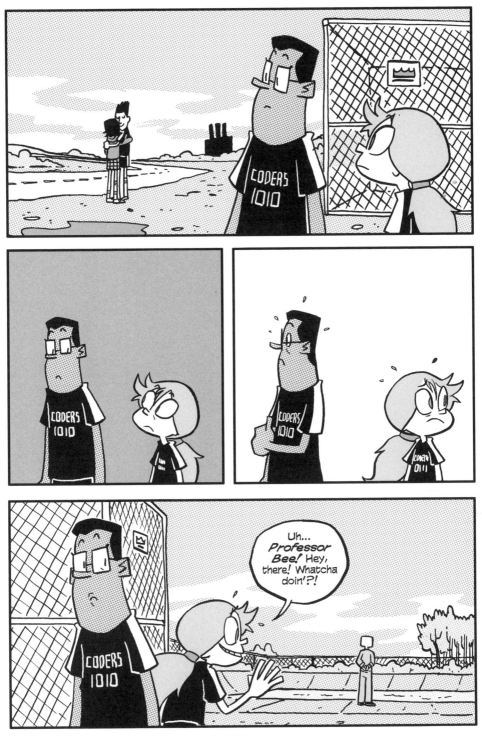

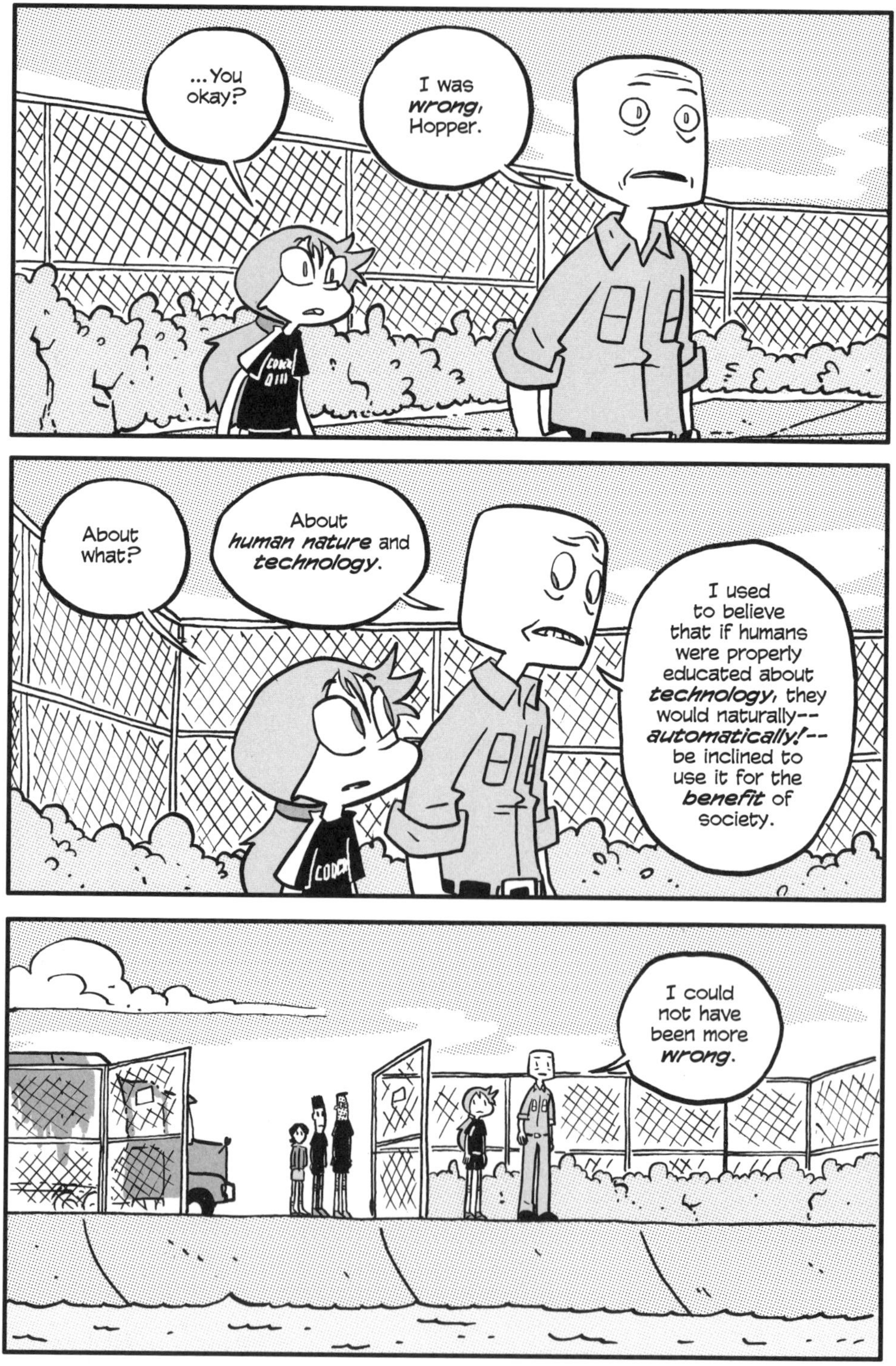
...You okay?
I was *wrong*, Hopper.
About what?
About *human nature* and *technology*.
I used to believe that if humans were properly educated about *technology*, they would naturally-- *automatically!*-- be inclined to use it for the *benefit* of society.
I could not have been more *wrong*.

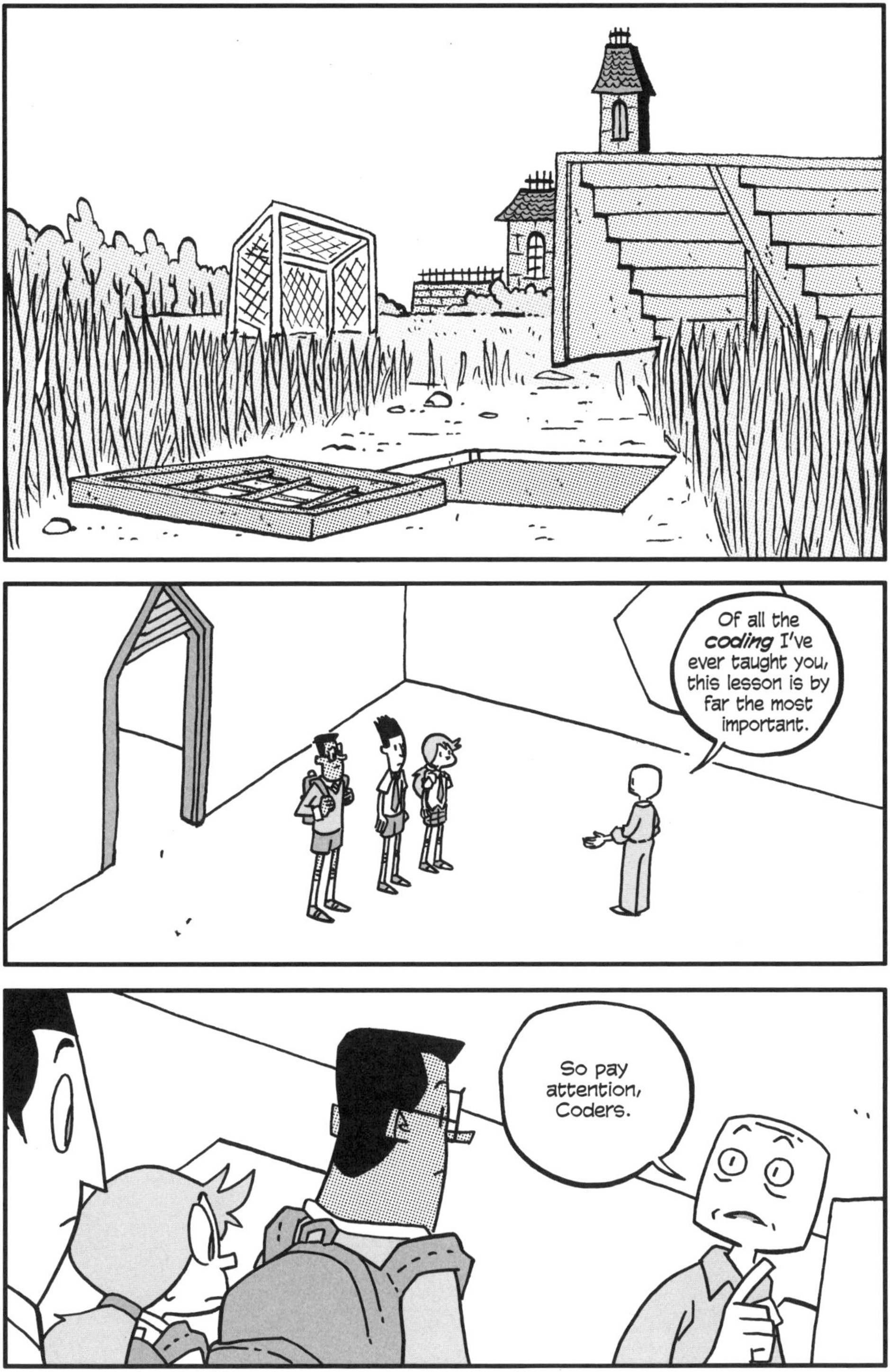
Of all the *coding* I've ever taught you, this lesson is by far the most important.
So pay attention, Coders.

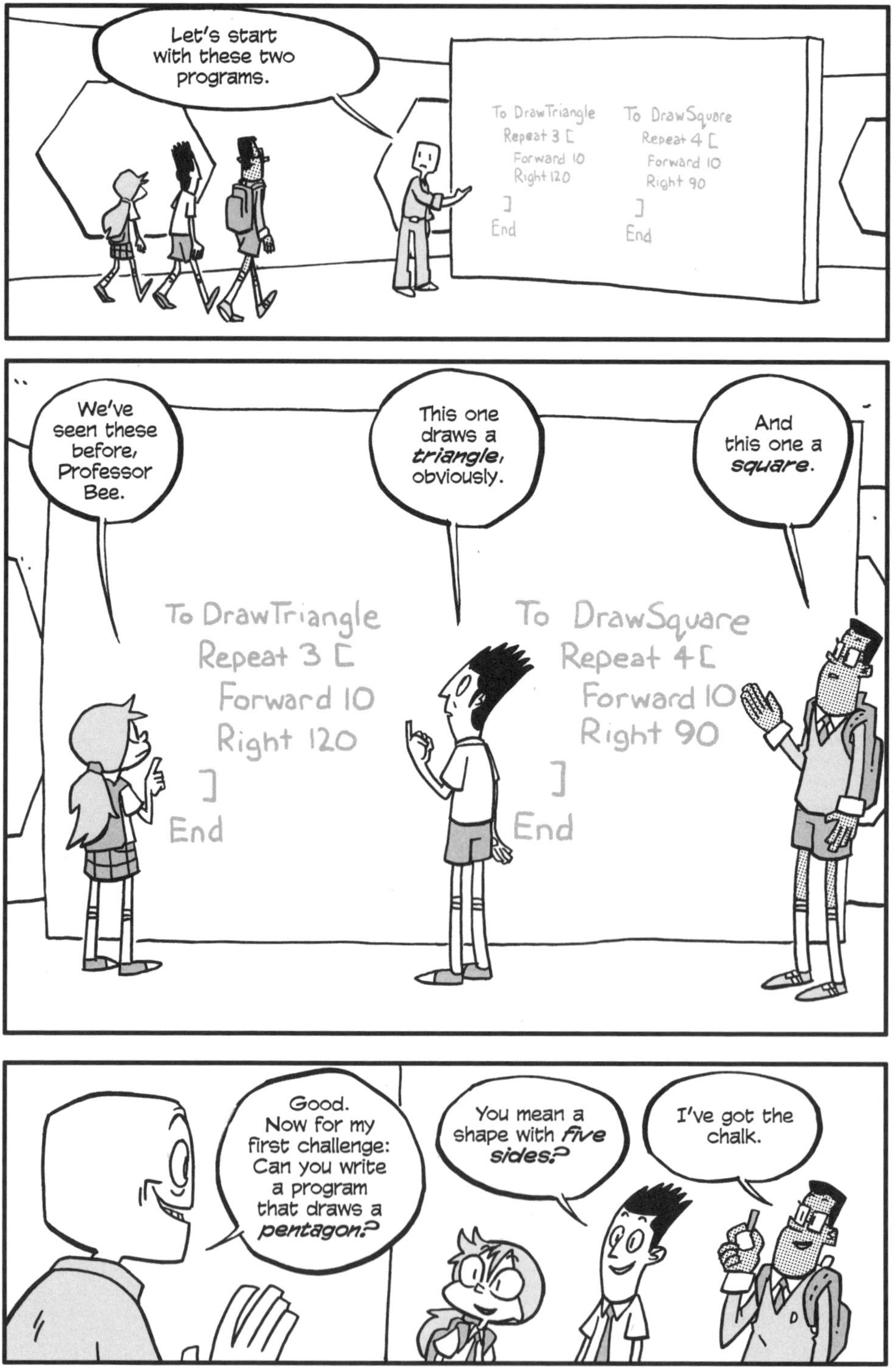

Let's start with these two programs.
To DrawTriangle
Repeat 3 [
Forward 10
Right 120
]
End
To DrawSquare
Repeat 4 [
Forward 10
Right 90
]
End
We've seen these before, Professor Bee.
This one draws a *triangle,* obviously.
And this one a *square*.
Good. Now for my first challenge: Can you write a program that draws a *pentagon?*
You mean a shape with *five sides?*
I've got the chalk.

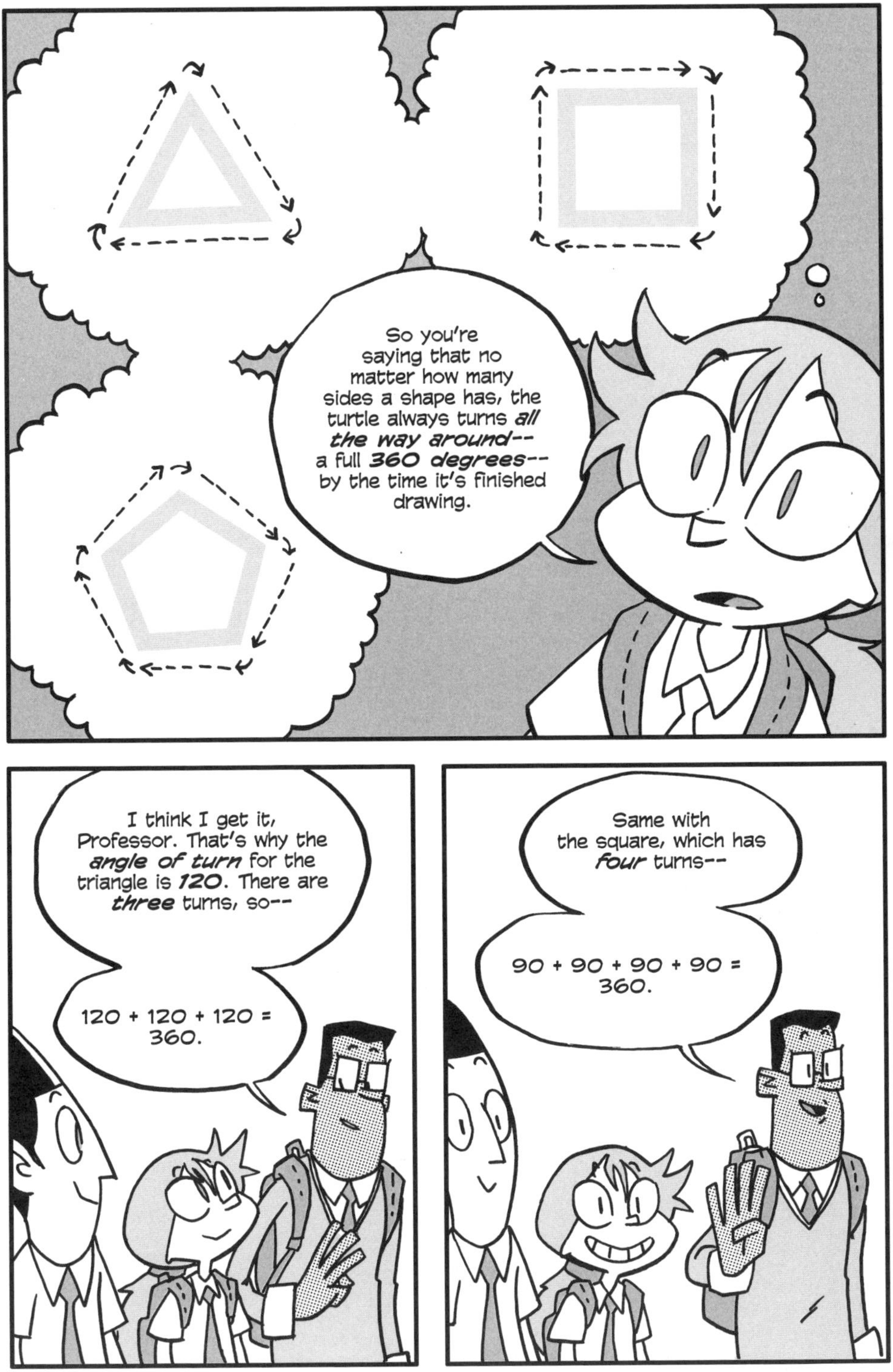
So you're saying that no matter how many sides a shape has, the turtle always turns *all the way around*-- a full *360 degrees*-- by the time it's finished drawing.
I think I get it, Professor. That's why the *angle of turn* for the triangle is *120*. There are *three* turns, so--
120 + 120 + 120 = 360.
Same with the square, which has *four* turns--
90 + 90 + 90 + 90 = 360.

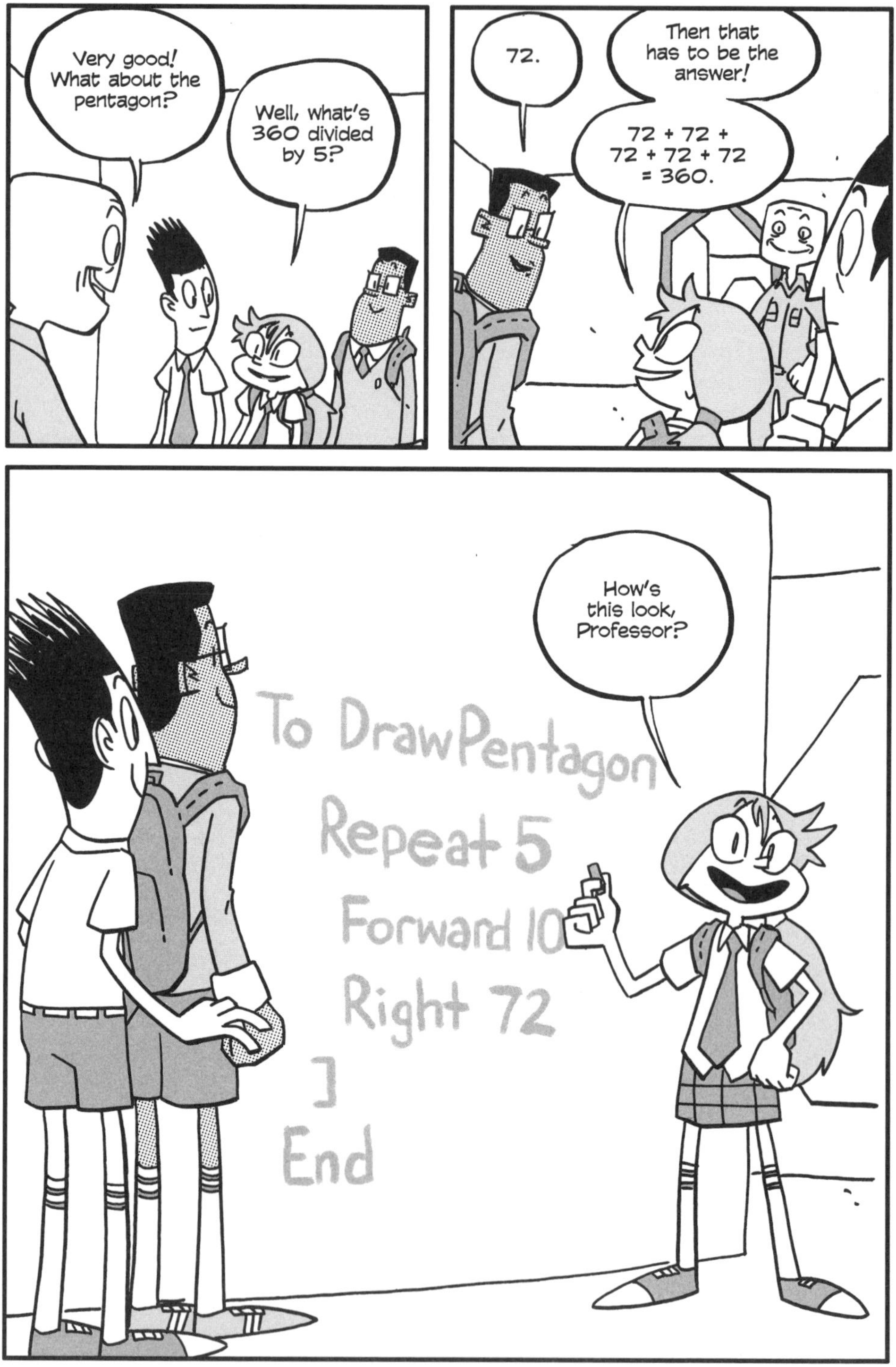
Very good! What about the pentagon?
Well, what's 360 divided by 5?
72.
72 + 72 + 72 + 72 + 72 = 360.
Then that has to be the answer!
How's this look, Professor?
To DrawPentagon
Repeat 5
Forward 10
Right 72
]
End

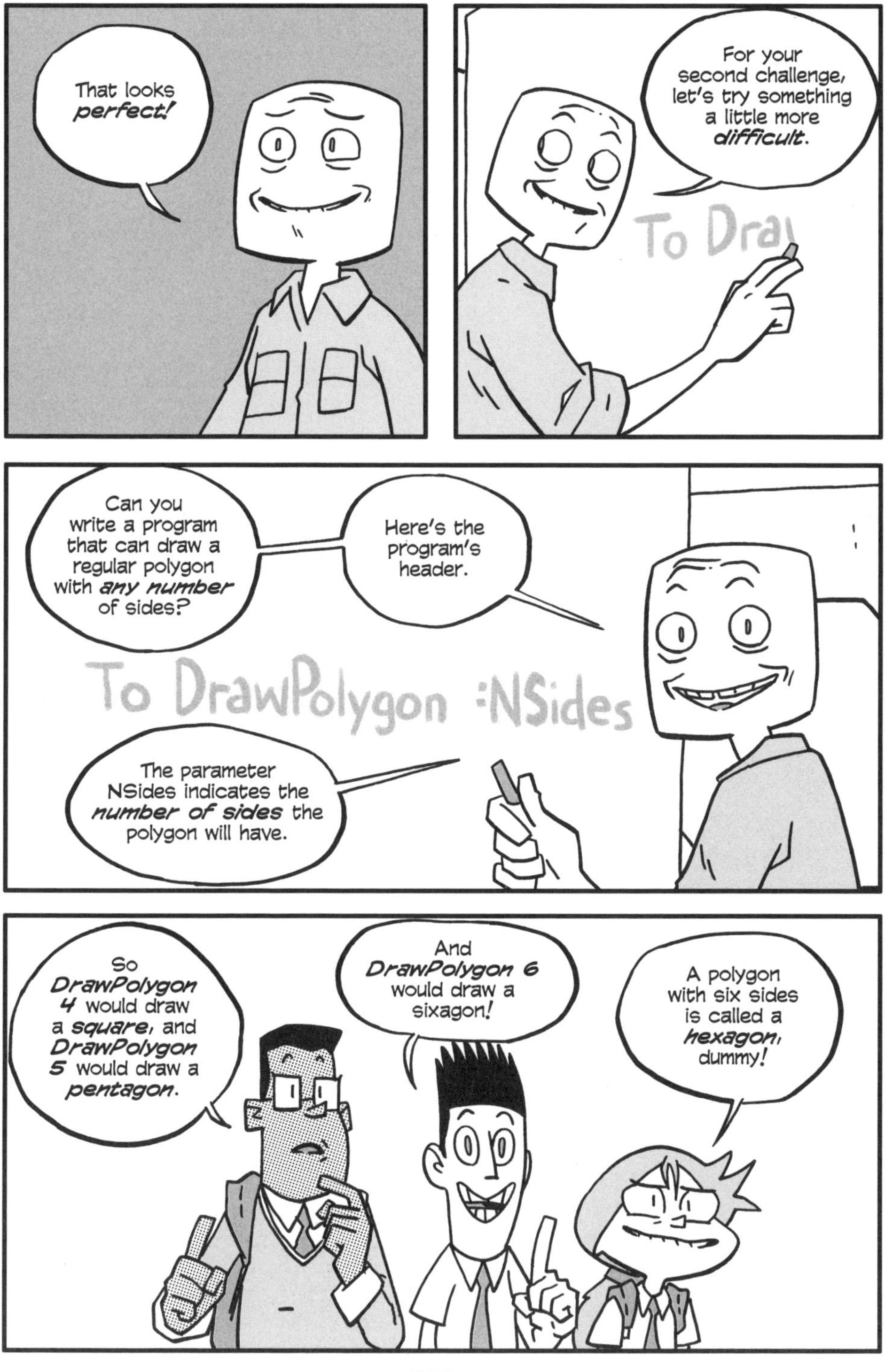
That looks *perfect!*
For your second challenge, let's try something a little more *difficult*.
To Dra
Can you write a program that can draw a regular polygon with *any number* of sides?
Here's the program's header.
To DrawPolygon :NSides
The parameter NSides indicates the *number of sides* the polygon will have.
So *DrawPolygon 4* would draw a *square*, and *DrawPolygon 5* would draw a *pentagon*.
And *DrawPolygon 6* would draw a sixagon!
A polygon with six sides is called a *hexagon*, dummy!

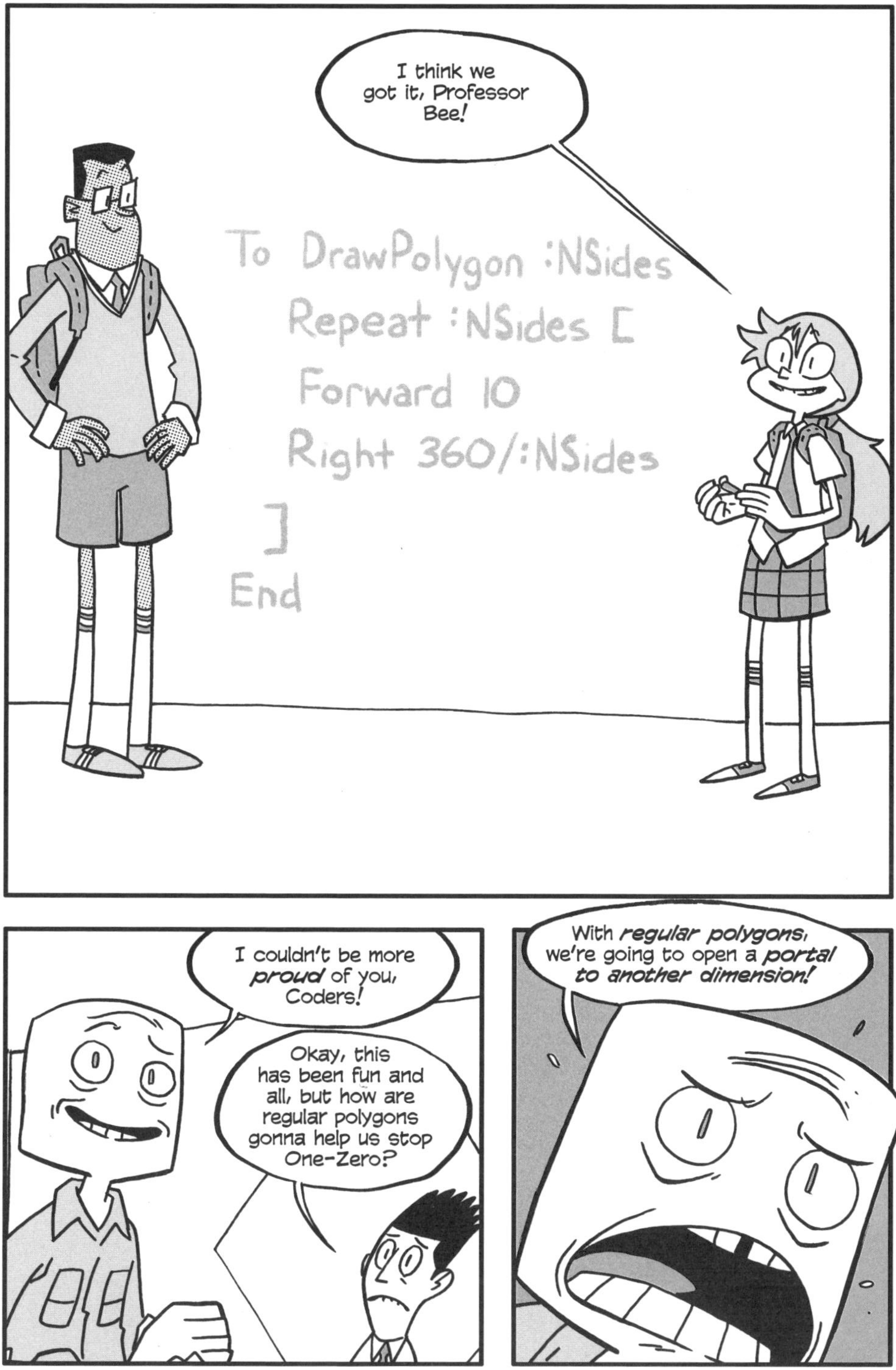
I think we got it, Professor Bee!
To DrawPolygon :NSides
Repeat :NSides [
Forward 10
Right 360/:NSides
]
End
I couldn't be more *proud* of you, Coders!
Okay, this has been fun and all, but how are regular polygons gonna help us stop One-Zero?
With ***regular polygons***, we're going to open a ***portal to another dimension!***

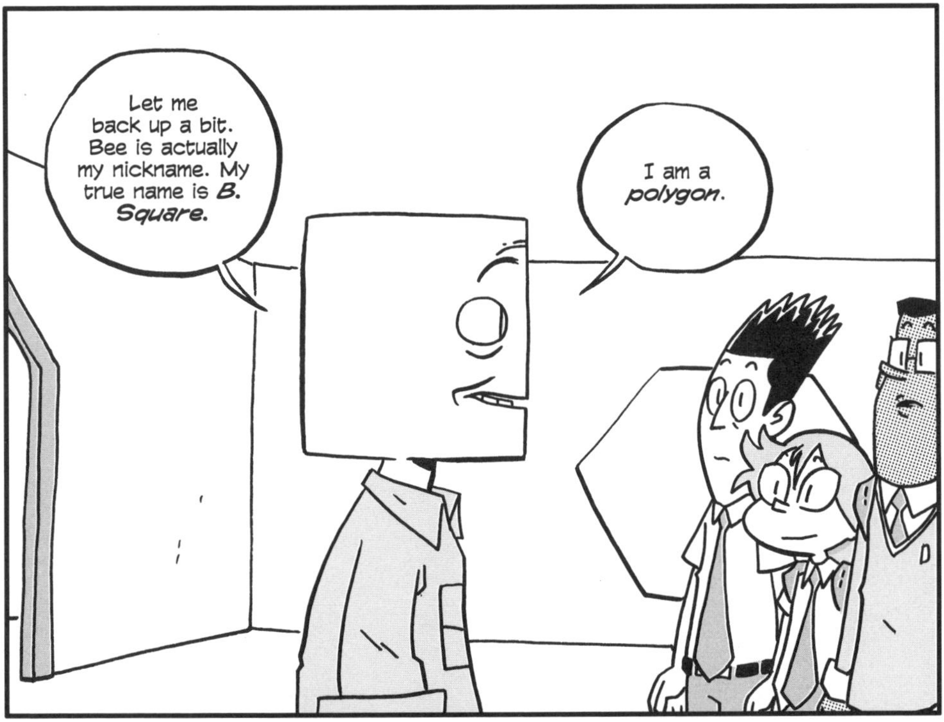
Let me back up a bit. Bee is actually my nickname. My true name is *B. Square.*
I am a *polygon*.

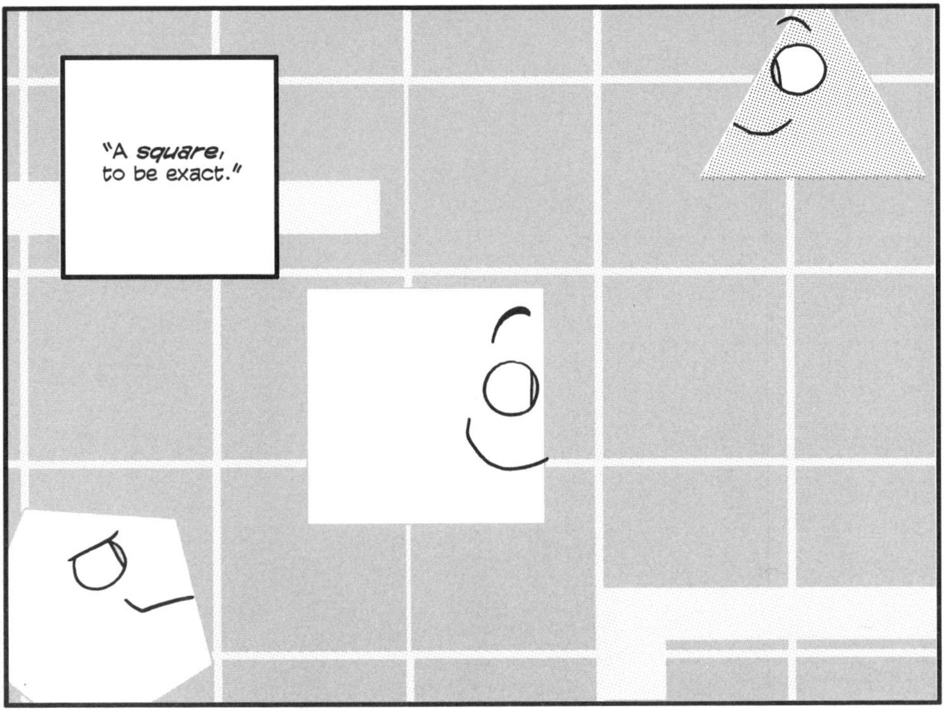
"A *square*, to be exact."

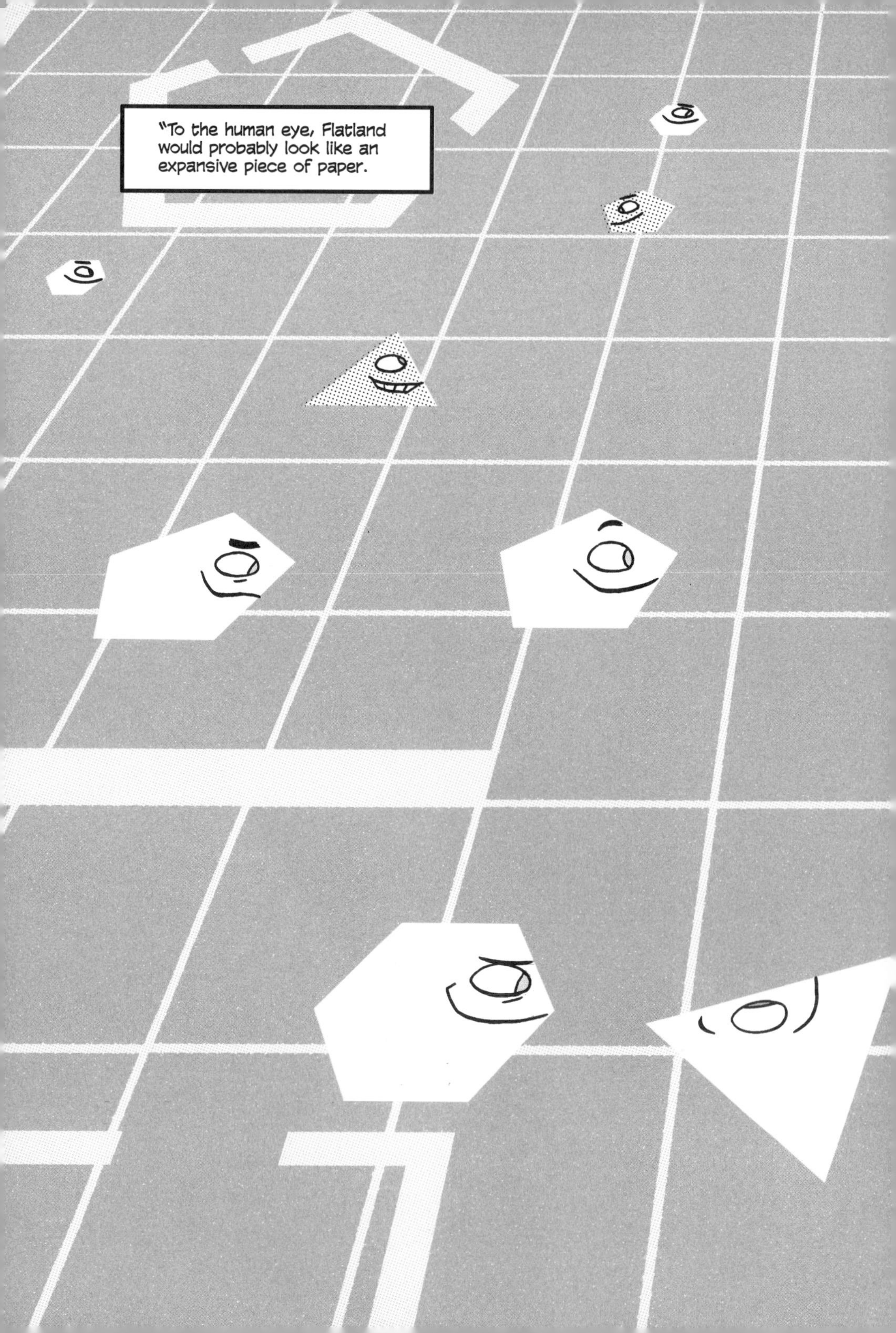
"To the human eye, Flatland would probably look like an expansive piece of paper.

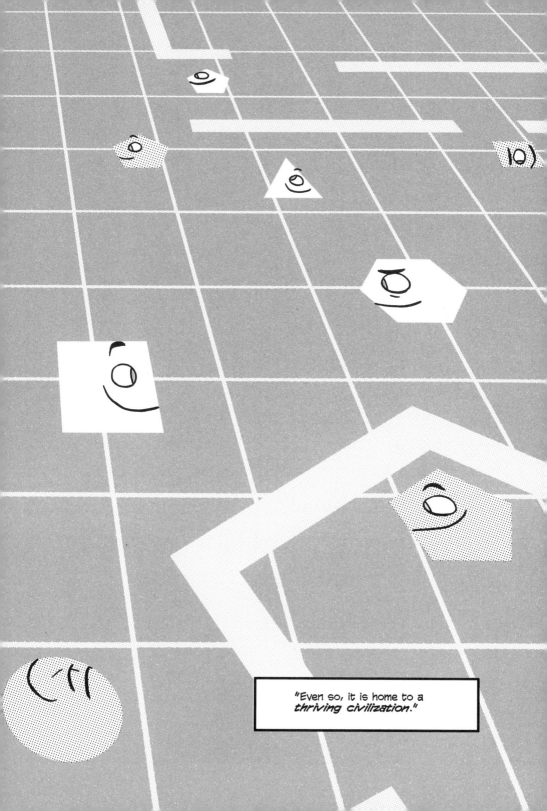

"Even so, it is home to a *thriving civilization.*"

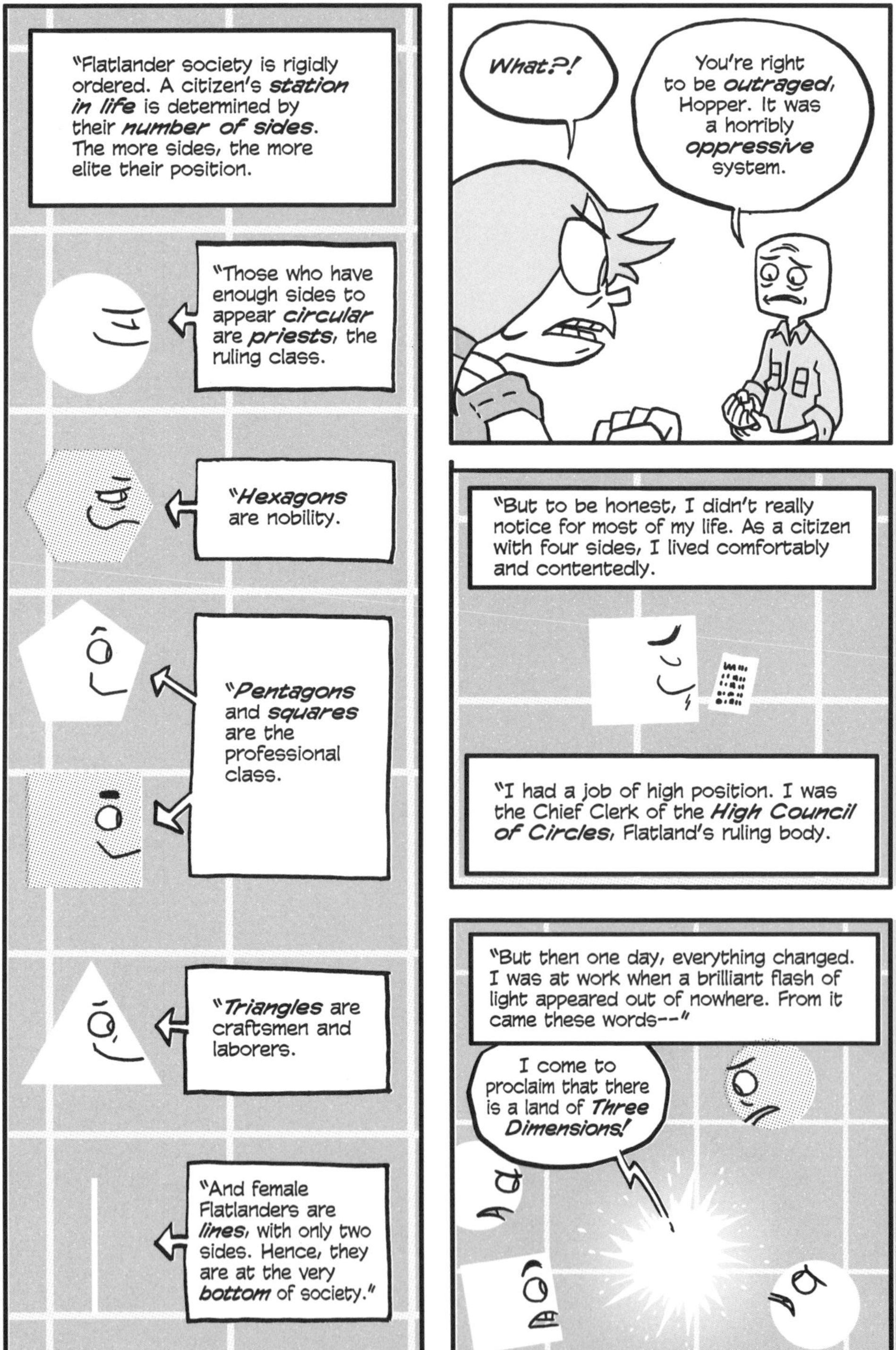

"Flatlander society is rigidly ordered. A citizen's *station in life* is determined by their *number of sides*. The more sides, the more elite their position.
"Those who have enough sides to appear *circular* are *priests*, the ruling class.
"*Hexagons* are nobility.
"*Pentagons* and *squares* are the professional class.
"*Triangles* are craftsmen and laborers.
"And female Flatlanders are *lines*, with only two sides. Hence, they are at the very *bottom* of society."
What?!
You're right to be *outraged*, Hopper. It was a horribly *oppressive* system.
"But to be honest, I didn't really notice for most of my life. As a citizen with four sides, I lived comfortably and contentedly.
"I had a job of high position. I was the Chief Clerk of the *High Council of Circles*, Flatland's ruling body.
"But then one day, everything changed. I was at work when a brilliant flash of light appeared out of nowhere. From it came these words--"
I come to proclaim that there is a land of *Three Dimensions!*

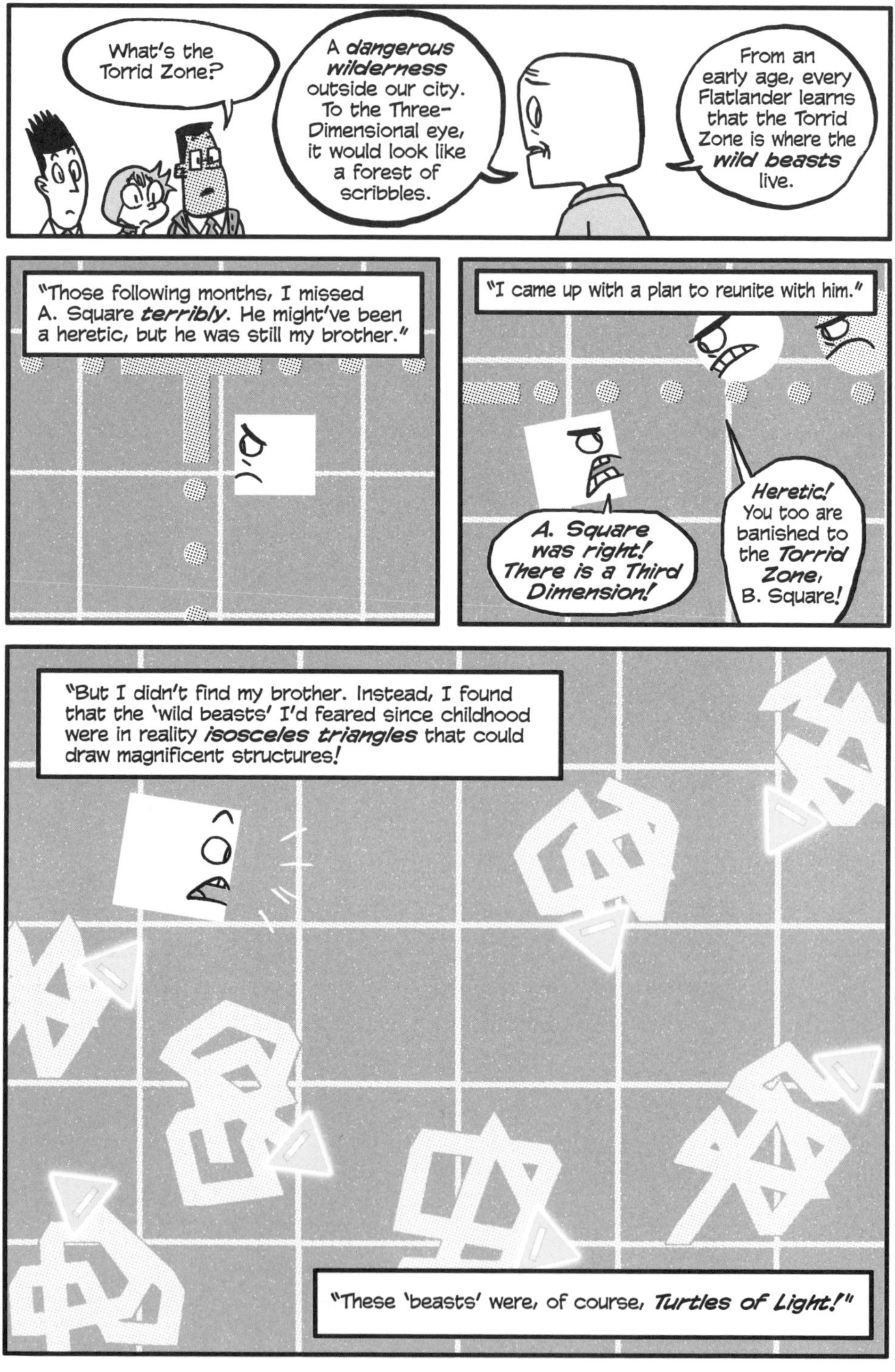
What's the Torrid Zone?
A *dangerous wilderness* outside our city. To the Three-Dimensional eye, it would look like a forest of scribbles.
From an early age, every Flatlander learns that the Torrid Zone is where the *wild beasts* live.
"Those following months, I missed A. Square *terribly*. He might've been a heretic, but he was still my brother."
"I came up with a plan to reunite with him."
A. Square was right! There is a Third Dimension!
Heretic! You too are banished to the *Torrid Zone*, B. Square!
"But I didn't find my brother. Instead, I found that the 'wild beasts' I'd feared since childhood were in reality *isosceles triangles* that could draw magnificent structures!
"These 'beasts' were, of course, *Turtles of Light!*"

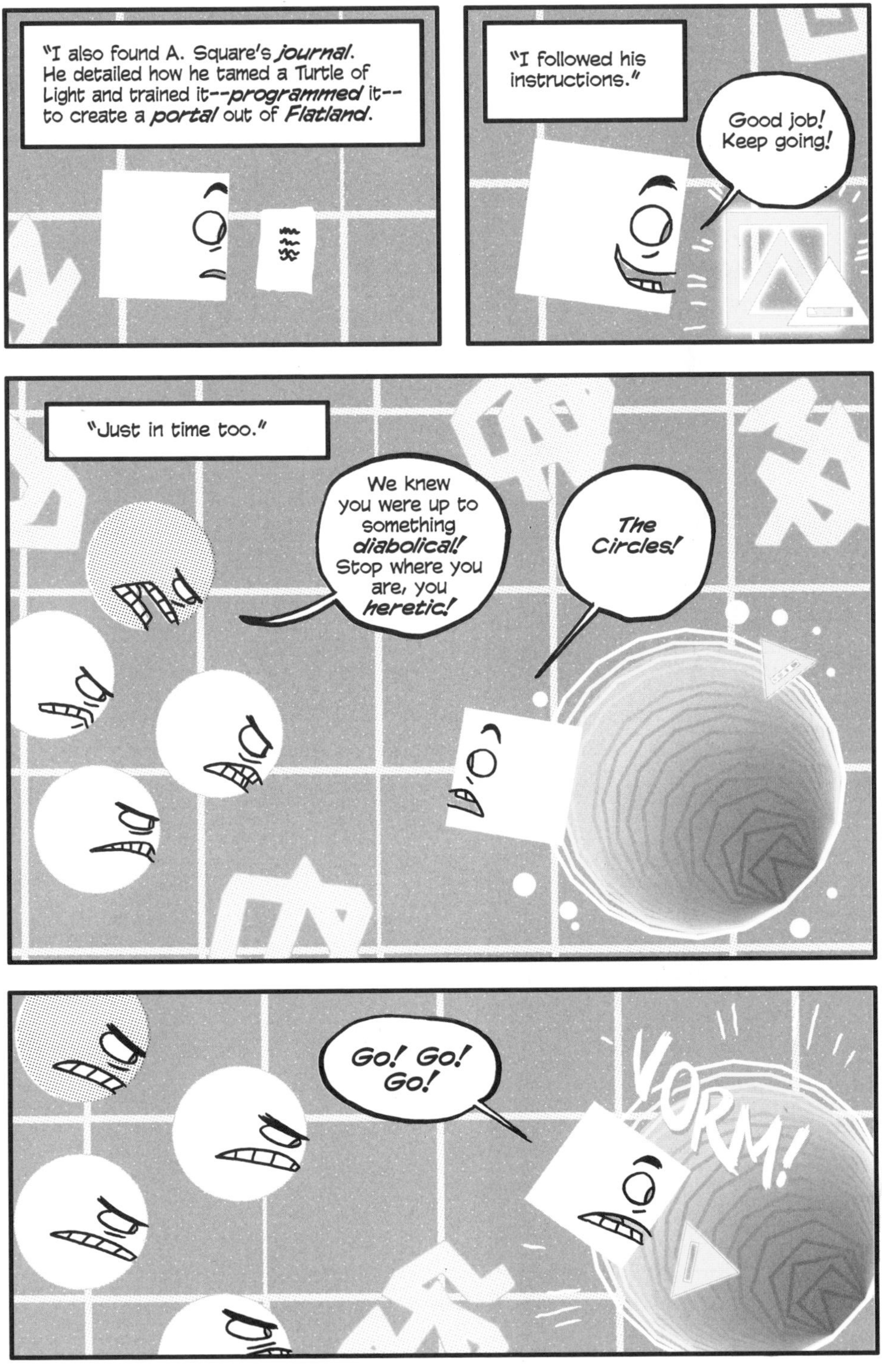
"I also found A. Square's *journal*. He detailed how he tamed a Turtle of Light and trained it--*programmed* it--to create a *portal* out of *Flatland*.
"I followed his instructions."
Good job! Keep going!
"Just in time too."
We knew you were up to something *diabolical!* Stop where you are, you *heretic!*
The Circles!
Go! Go! Go!
VORM!

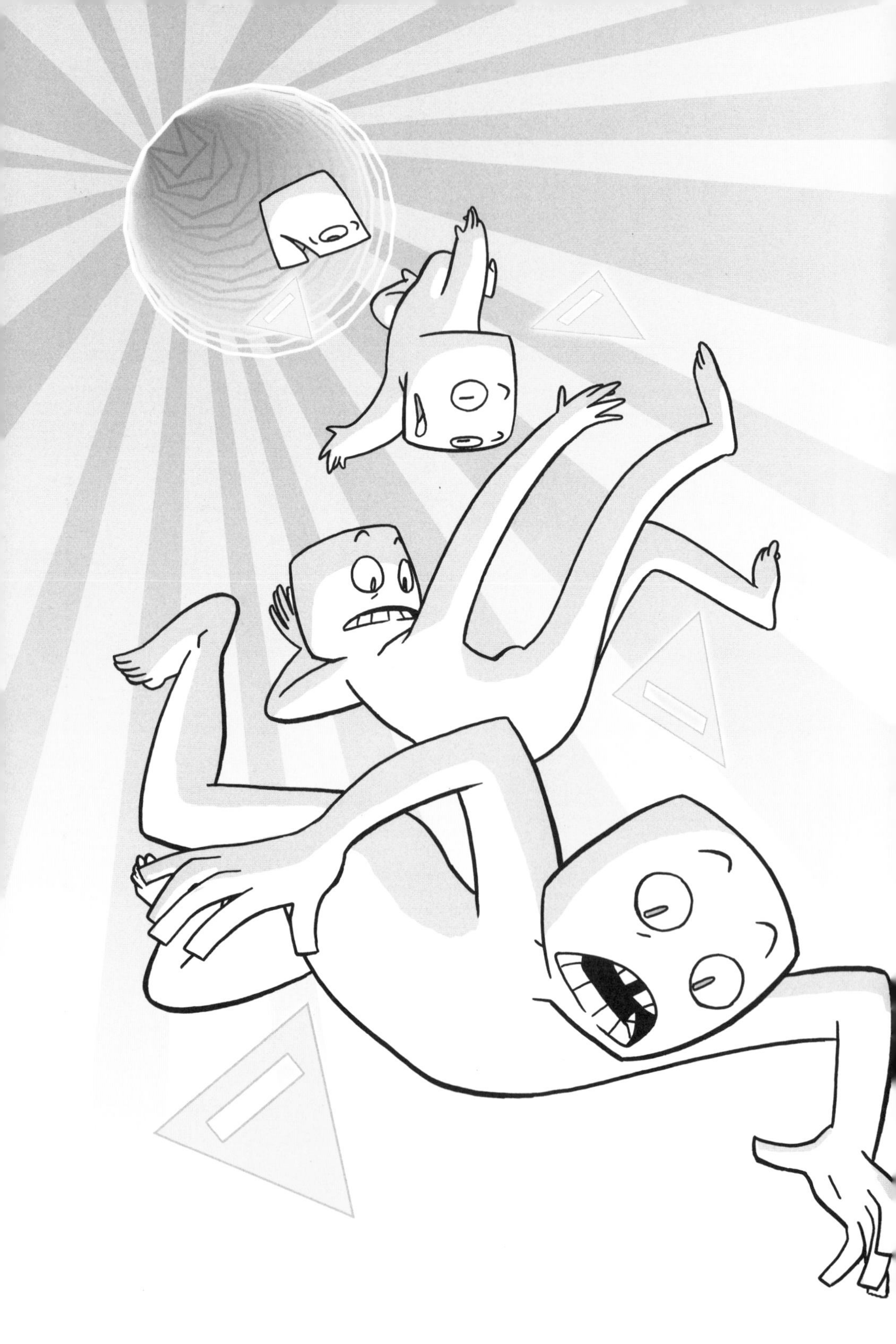

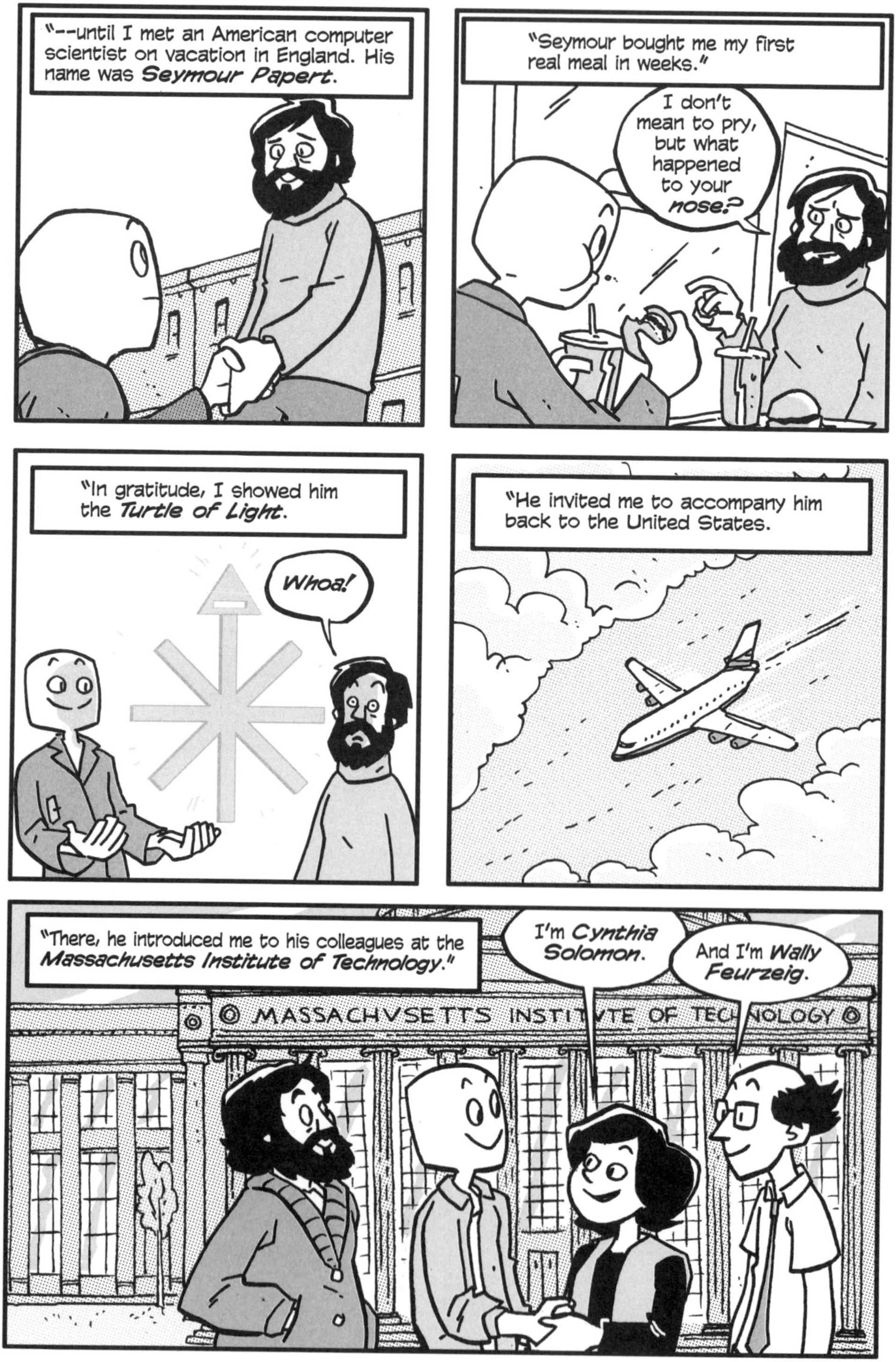
"--until I met an American computer scientist on vacation in England. His name was *Seymour Papert*.
"Seymour bought me my first real meal in weeks."
I don't mean to pry, but what happened to your *nose?*
"In gratitude, I showed him the *Turtle of Light*.
Whoa!
"He invited me to accompany him back to the United States.
"There, he introduced me to his colleagues at the *Massachusetts Institute of Technology*."
I'm *Cynthia Solomon*.
And I'm *Wally Feurzeig*.
MASSACHVSETTS INSTITVTE OF TECHNOLOGY

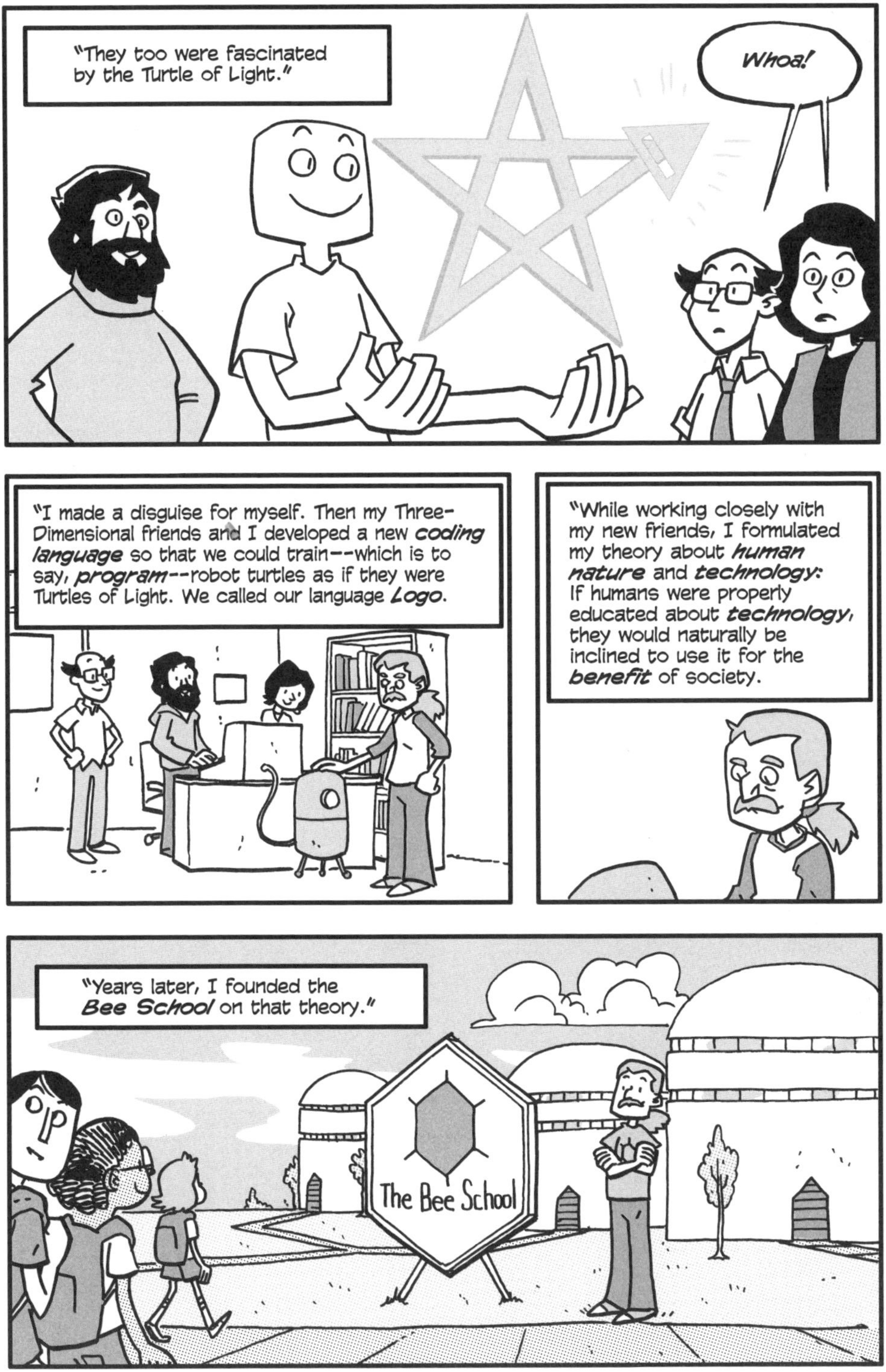
"They too were fascinated by the Turtle of Light."
Whoa!
"I made a disguise for myself. Then my Three-Dimensional friends and I developed a new coding language so that we could train--which is to say, program--robot turtles as if they were Turtles of Light. We called our language Logo.
"While working closely with my new friends, I formulated my theory about human nature and technology: If humans were properly educated about technology, they would naturally be inclined to use it for the benefit of society.
"Years later, I founded the Bee School on that theory."
The Bee School

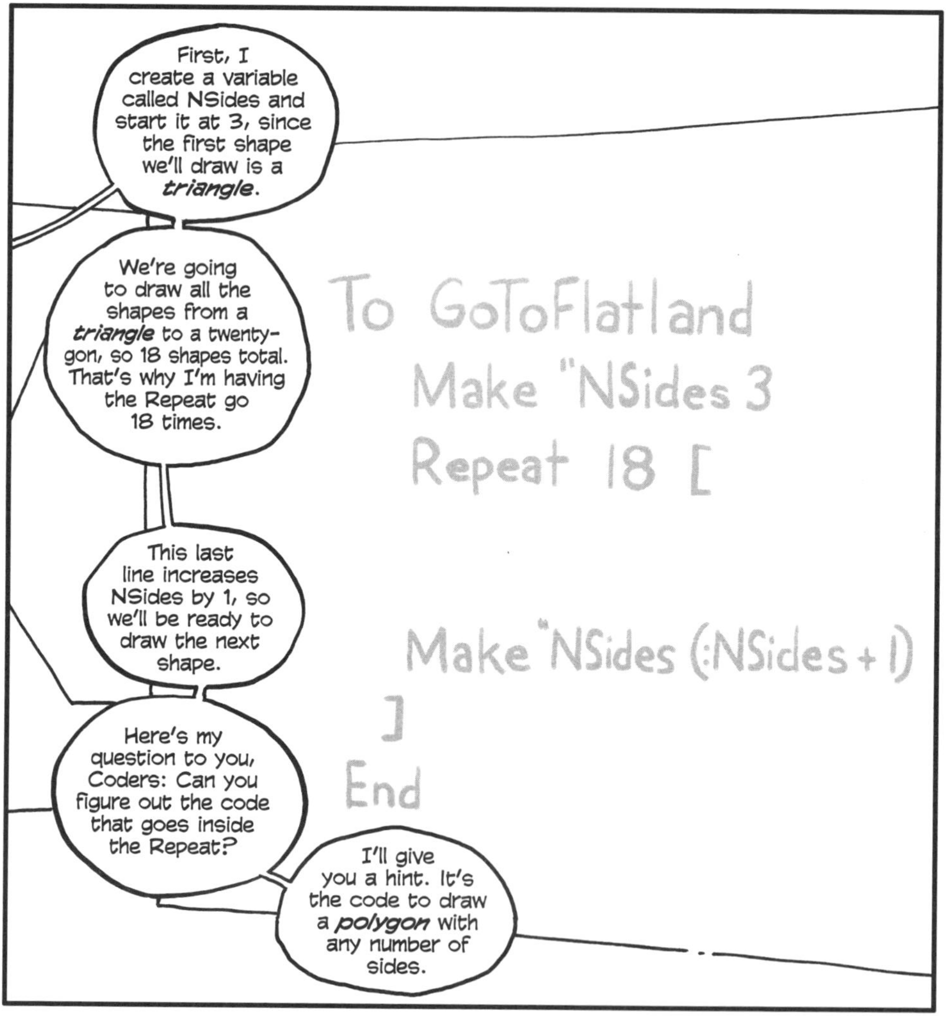
First, I create a variable called NSides and start it at 3, since the first shape we'll draw is a *triangle*.
We're going to draw all the shapes from a *triangle* to a twenty-gon, so 18 shapes total. That's why I'm having the Repeat go 18 times.
This last line increases NSides by 1, so we'll be ready to draw the next shape.
Here's my question to you, Coders: Can you figure out the code that goes inside the Repeat?
I'll give you a hint. It's the code to draw a *polygon* with any number of sides.
To GoToFlatland
Make "NSides 3
Repeat 18 [
Make "NSides (:NSides + 1)
]
End

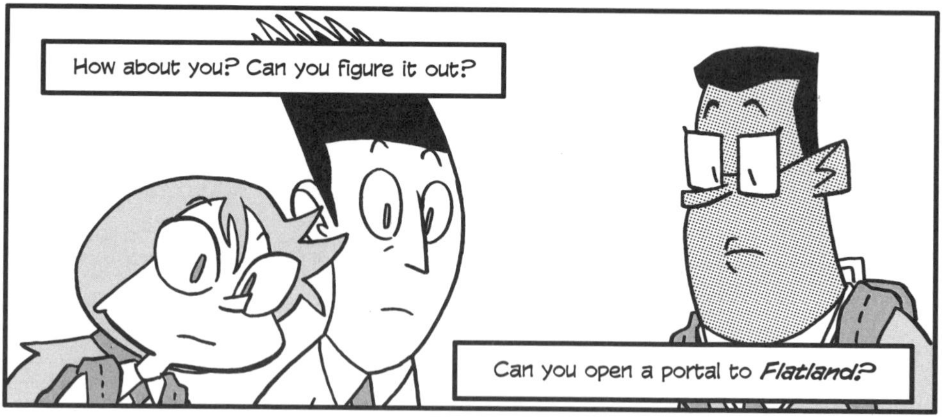
How about you? Can you figure it out?
Can you open a portal to *Flatland?*

Continued in

SECRET CODERS

Monsters & Modules

Ready to start coding?

Visit www.secret-coders.com

Check out these other books
in the Secret Coders series!

**Secret Coders
Paths & Portals
Secrets & Sequences
Robots & Repeats**

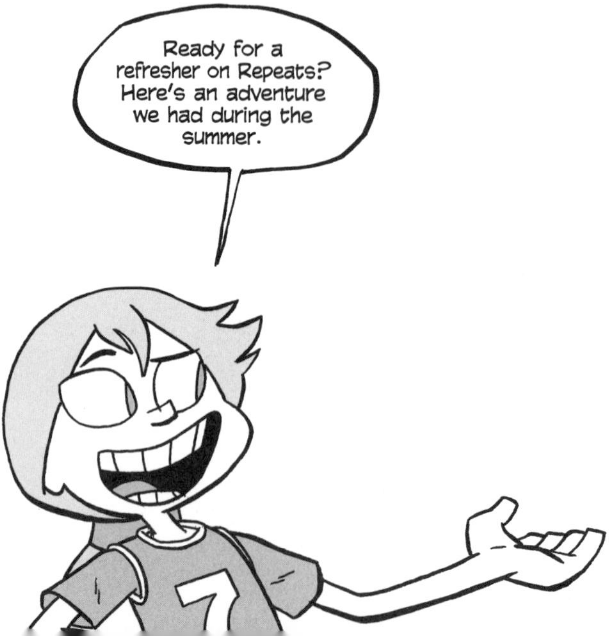
Ready for a refresher on Repeats? Here's an adventure we had during the summer.

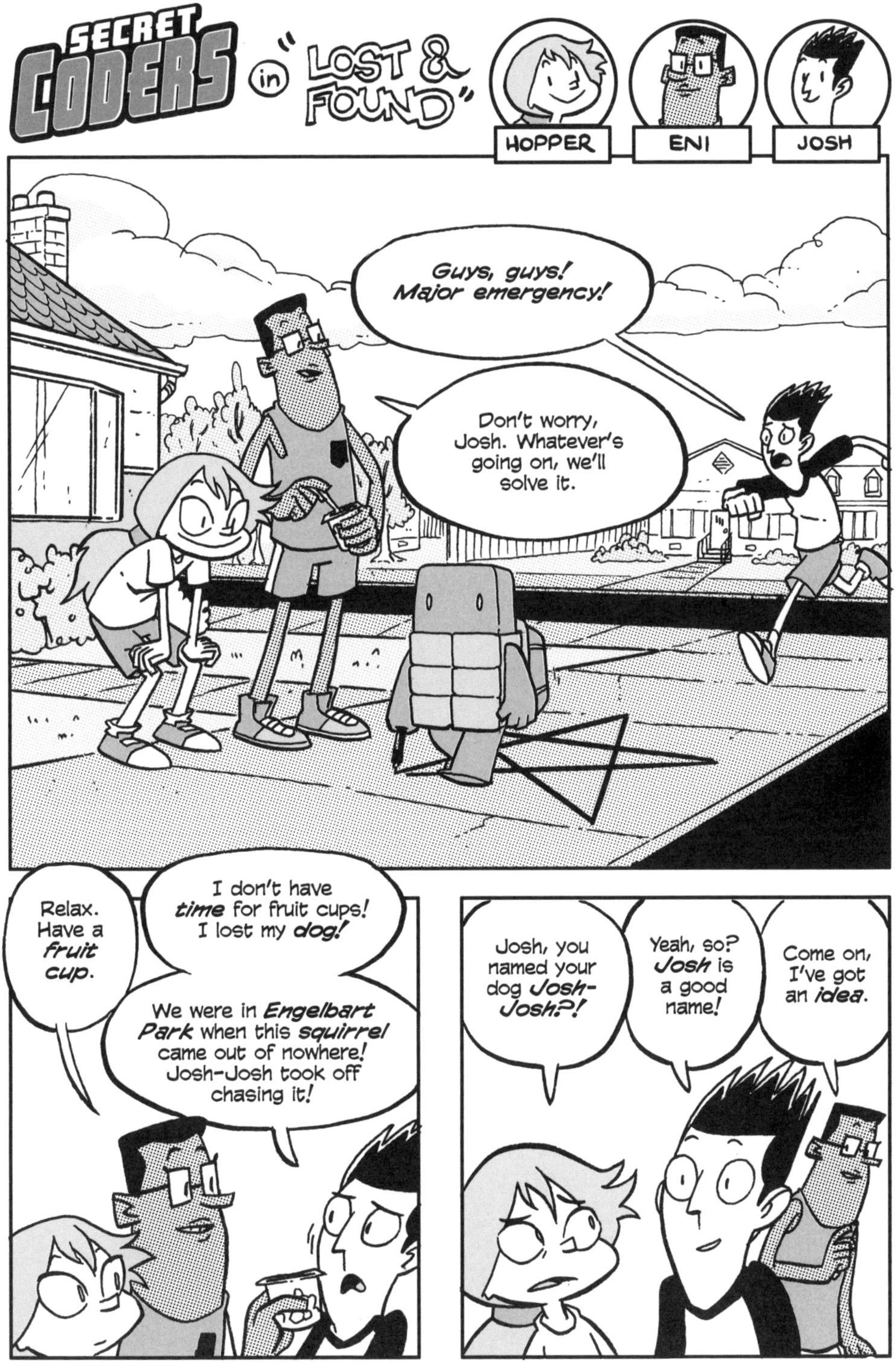
SECRET CODERS in "LOST & FOUND"
HOPPER
ENI
JOSH
Guys, guys! Major emergency!
Don't worry, Josh. Whatever's going on, we'll solve it.
Relax. Have a fruit cup.
I don't have time for fruit cups! I lost my dog!
We were in Engelbart Park when this squirrel came out of nowhere! Josh-Josh took off chasing it!
Josh, you named your dog Josh-Josh?!
Yeah, so? Josh is a good name!
Come on, I've got an idea.

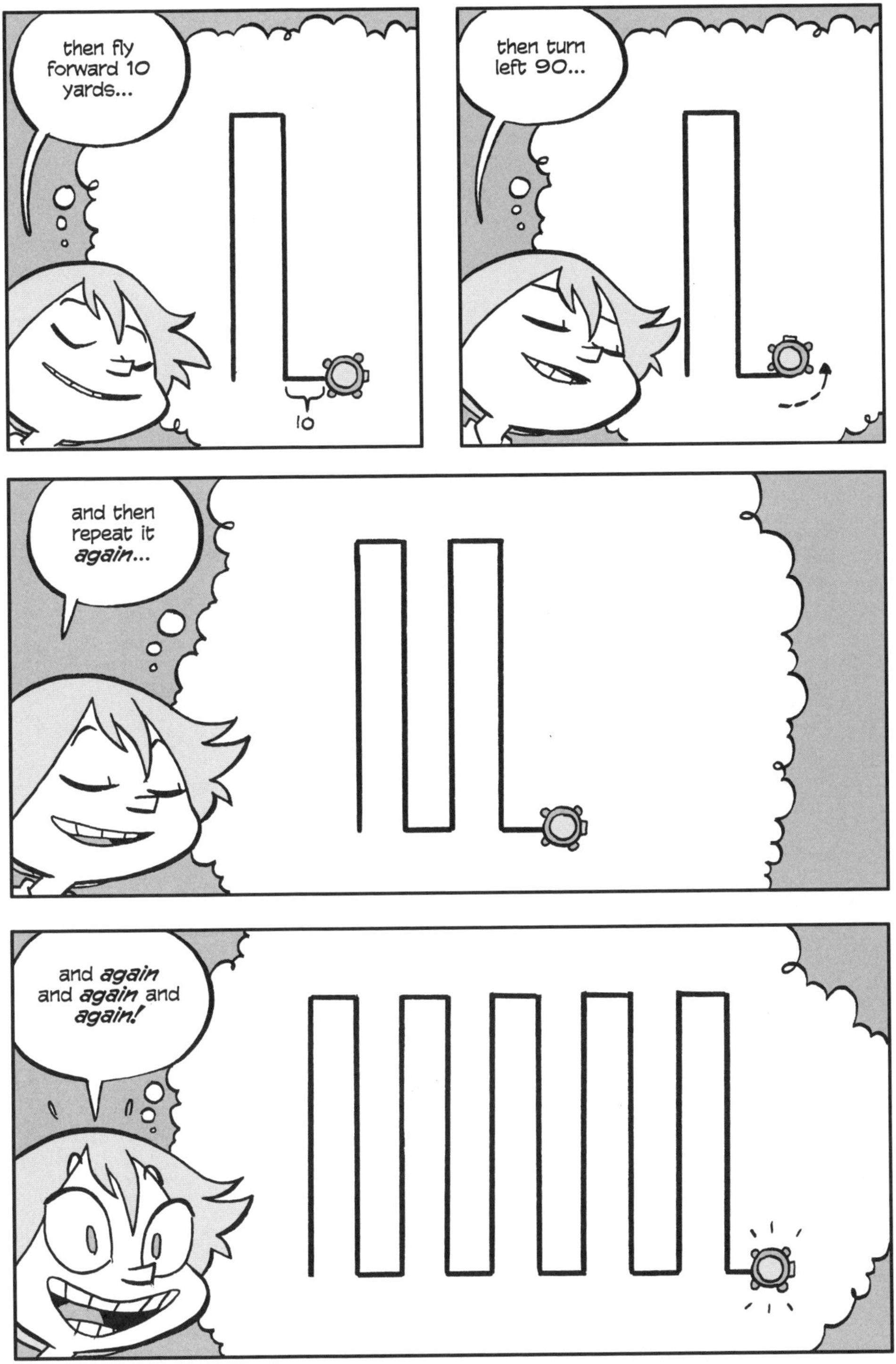
then fly forward 10 yards...
10
then turn left 90...
and then repeat it *again*...
and *again* and *again* and *again!*

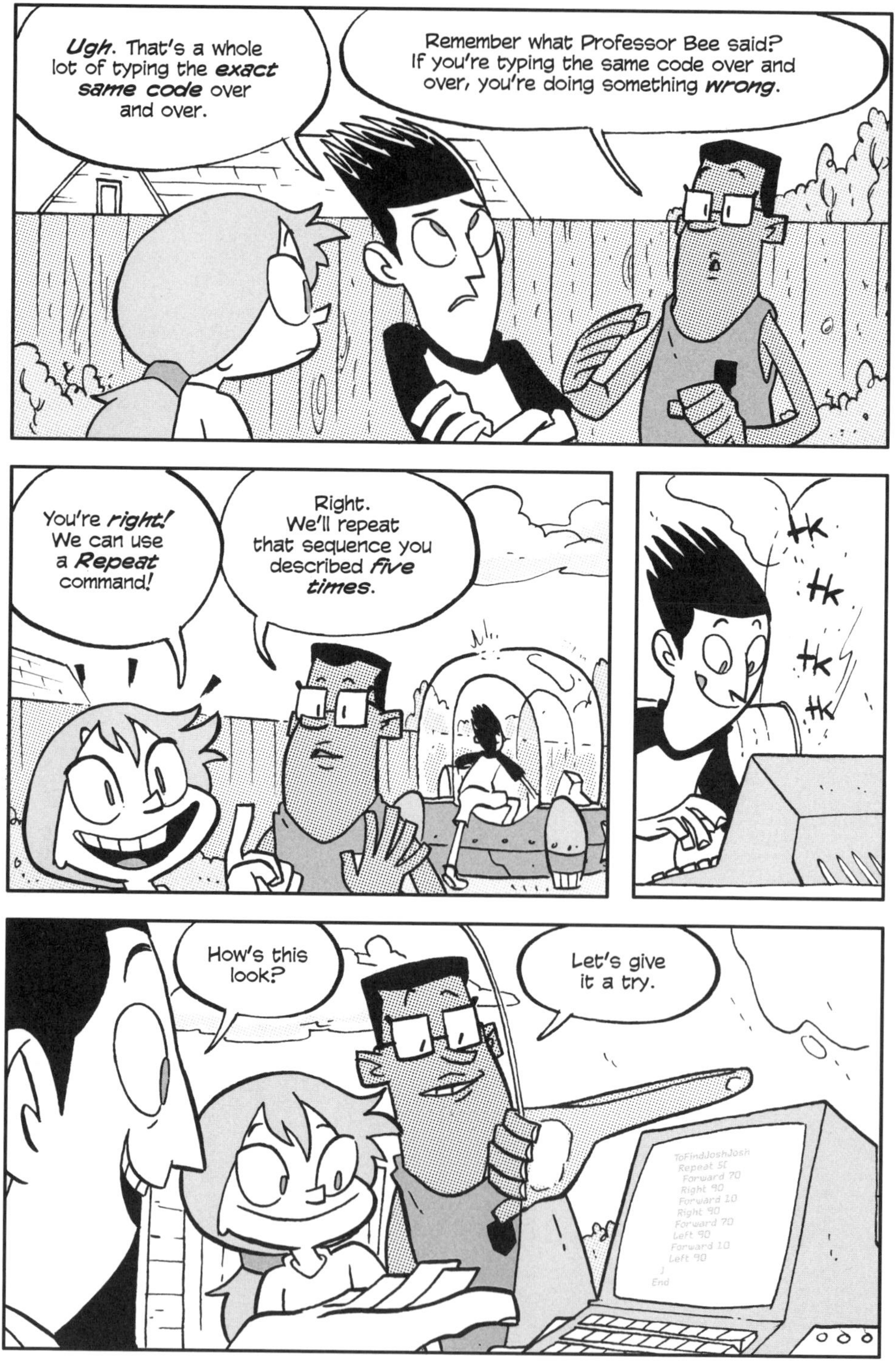

Ugh. That's a whole lot of typing the ***exact same code*** over and over.
Remember what Professor Bee said? If you're typing the same code over and over, you're doing something ***wrong***.
You're ***right!*** We can use a ***Repeat*** command!
Right. We'll repeat that sequence you described ***five times***.
tk
tk
tk
tk
How's this look?
Let's give it a try.
ToFindJoshJosh
Repeat 5[
Forward 70
Right 90
Forward 10
Right 90
Forward 70
Left 90
Forward 10
Left 90
]
End

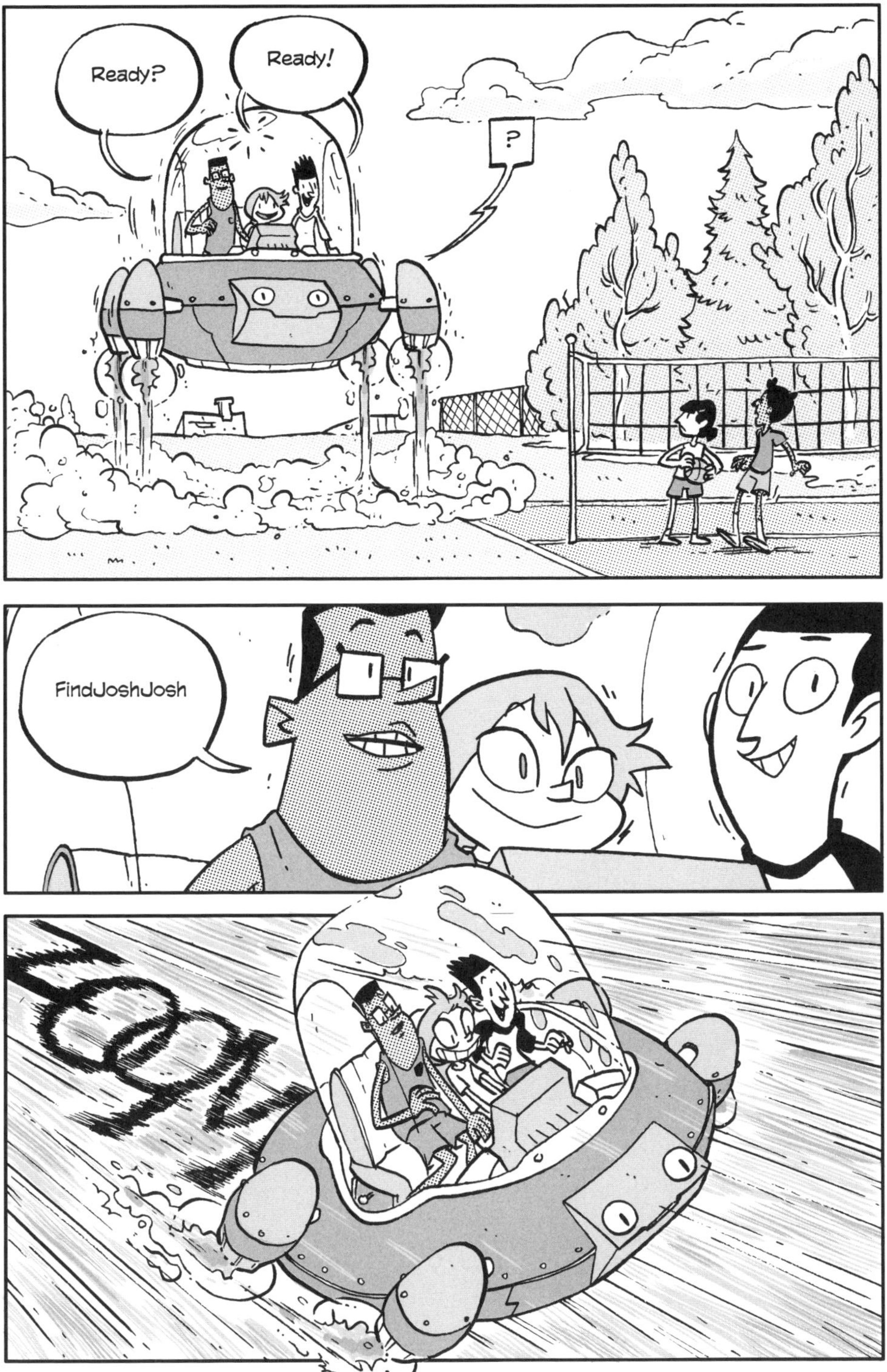
Ready?
Ready!
?
FindJoshJosh

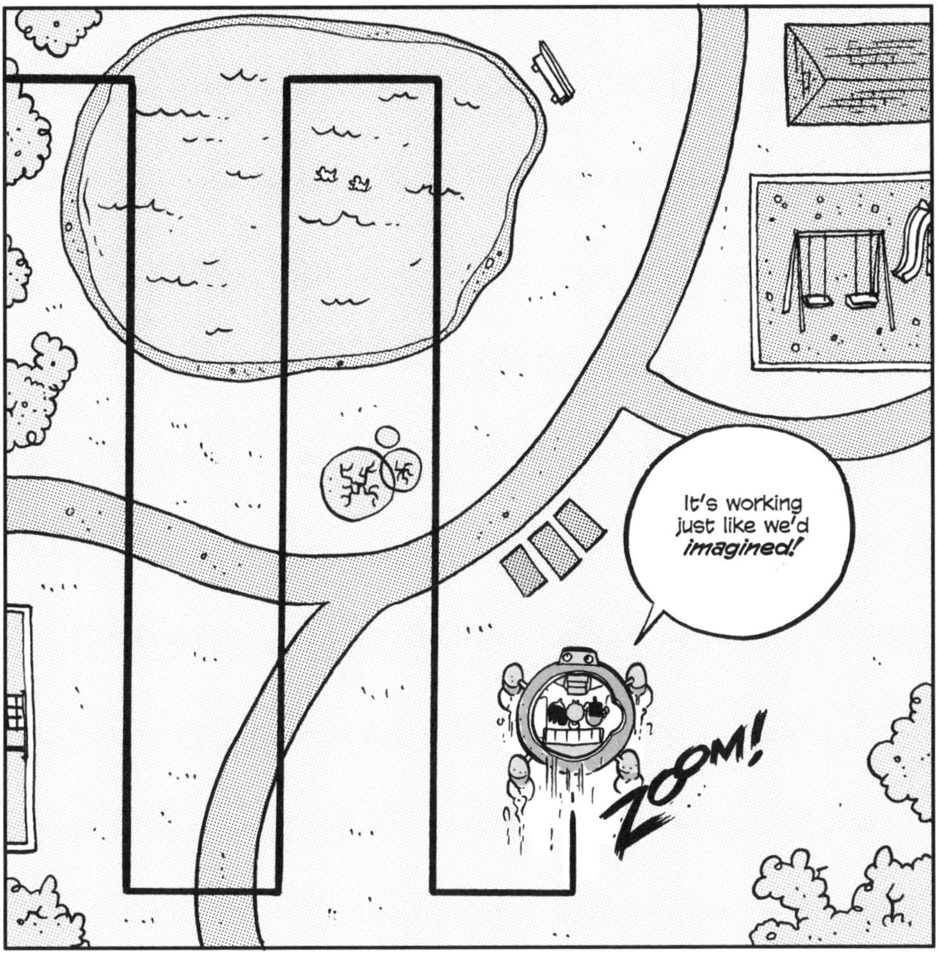
It's working just like we'd *imagined!*
ZOOM!

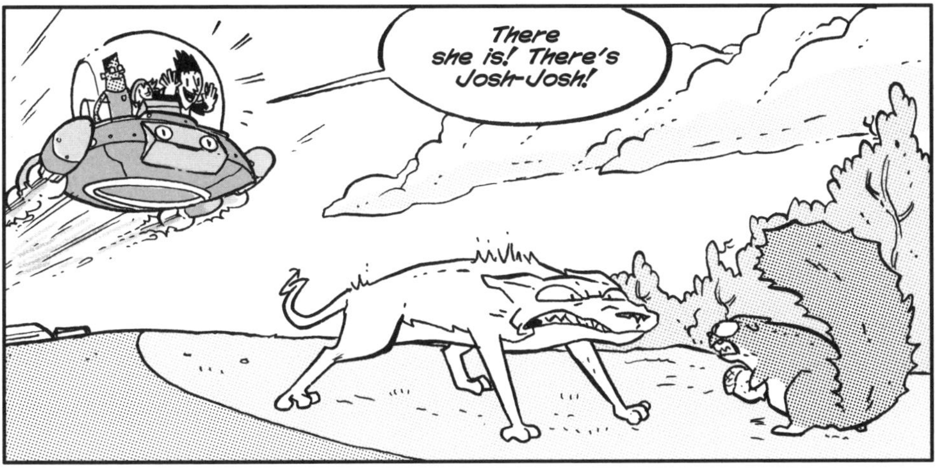
There she is! There's Josh-Josh!

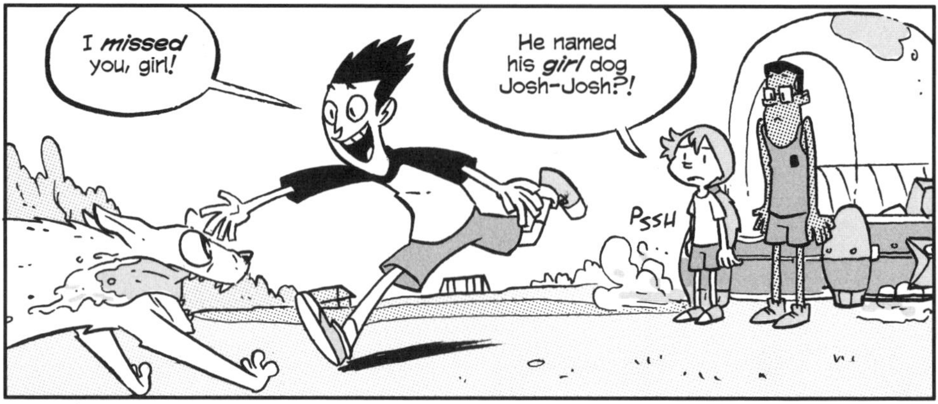
I *missed* you, girl!
He named his *girl* dog Josh-Josh?!
PSSH

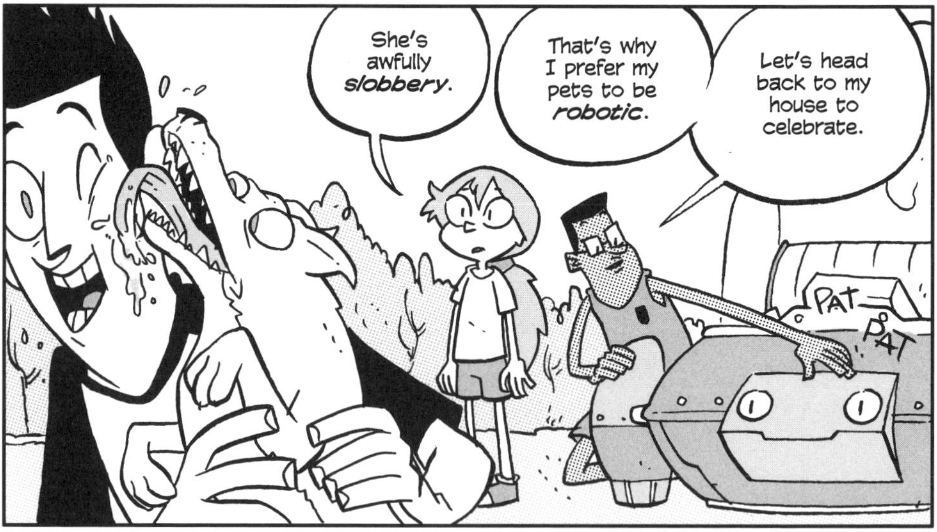
She's awfully *slobbery*.
That's why I prefer my pets to be *robotic*.
Let's head back to my house to celebrate.
PAT PAT

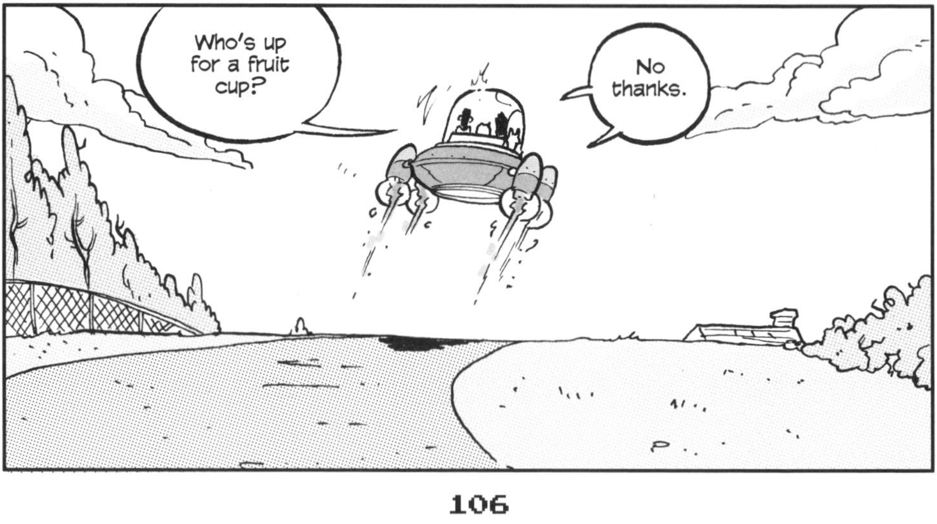
Who's up for a fruit cup?
No thanks.

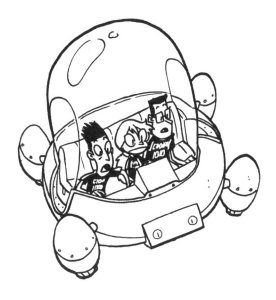

Thank you to Mike for being such an awesome partner on this project; to my wife and kids for being my first beta readers; to the First Second Books team—Simon Boughton, Mark Siegel, Calista Brill, Gina Gagliano, Robyn Chapman, Kiara Valdez, Danielle Ceccolini, and Andrew Arnold—for creating a home for stories; to Judy Hansen for her wisdom and guidance, and to every student who has ever set foot in my computer lab at Bishop O'Dowd High School for sharing my love of coding.

—Gene

As always and forever, I want to thank my wife, Meredith— you make my life and my work a lot more meaningful. Thanks to my incredible nieces, Ruby and Gabby, who give me great feedback and let me draw with them. And to Gene, who is an incredible collaborator and inspiration.

—Mike

TAKE GENE LUEN YANG'S
READING WITHOUT WALLS
CHALLENGE

Read outside your comfort zone!

①

Read a book about a **character** who
doesn't look or live like you.

②

Read a book about a **topic** you
don't know much about.

③

Read a book in a **format** that you
don't normally read for fun.

Learn more at **ReadingWithoutWalls.com**

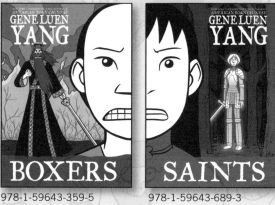